ARIELLA'S
REBELLION

BOOK TWO OF THE STARS AT ZENITH TRILOGY

CAROLEE CROFT

ISBN: 1775047938
ISBN-13: 978-1-7750479-3-3

Cover Art by Kellie Dennis at Book Cover by Design
www.bookcoverbydesign.co.uk

CONTENTS

Carolee Croft

ACKNOWLEDGMENTS

A big thank you again to Dallas Reagan for all your support and for reading the first draft. Also, the usual suspects: Shehanne Moore, Resa McConaghy, Mike Steeden, George aka Zoolon, Christy Birmingham, Aquileana, and R.K. Lander.

Futile – the winds –
To a heart in port –
Done with the compass –
Done with the chart!

- Emily Dickinson

Ariella's Rebellion

CHAPTER 1

The ringing of steel echoed through the open courtyard as Ariella trained, battling Jaquelle and having a damned difficult time of it too. Her former nursemaid and now swordplay instructor had obviously never heard of easing back into things.

It had been three weeks since her fateful duel with Ancarette. The wound had recently healed, but Ariella was not in good fighting shape after her prolonged rest. This was the first time she picked up a sword since that snow-speckled day on the field outside Castle Leduryon, where she had incurred the near mortal wound in her chest. Now, the muscles had been repaired thanks to Jaquelle's magical healing skill, but they were weak and stiff from disuse.

Jaquelle advanced, making Ariella retreat past several columns that supported the balconies encompassing the rectangle of the yard. The place had an air of abandonment. Servants passed unseen in the shadows of the balconies, their footsteps echoing loudly in the empty space. It was a remote wing of the castle to which Ariella was consigned so she would not be disturbed during her recovery, or maybe to keep her out of the way of the king and queen, whom she had still not met.

The winter of Sylcadia was so much milder than that of her

homeland, Dezearre. Although the air held a wet and cloying chill, Ariella no longer felt it. She was down to her shirt and light wool hose, sweating from the exercise. Her arms, chest, and back ached from the unaccustomed strain of wielding the sword, but Jaquelle kept up the rapid attack, taking them through all the classic lunges and parries. These were manageable, but Jaquelle then began to throw unexpected combinations at her until at last Ariella pleaded for mercy.

"A small respite," she cried, raising her hands and dropping her sword.

"Is this what you will say on the field of battle?" Jaquelle asked, but nevertheless lowered her sword.

Ariella drew a bucketful of water from the well that stood in the center of the courtyard. She drank deeply, and when she lowered the cup she felt someone's eyes on her. Up on the balcony stood a young woman. Unlike the servants who walked by occasionally glancing at the training bout, she was standing perfectly still, her arms spread wide gripping the railing. She was looking directly at Ariella. She wore simple riding boots, tight hose, and a tight jacket, all in black, all chosen no doubt to show off the graceful contours of her slim body.

Ariella's stomach gave a sickening lurch. She knew at once who this was.

The only way she could deal with this was to put on an air of bravado. "Good day," she offered.

The woman nodded but did not deign to reply. However, she moved from her post on the balcony and stalked purposefully down the stairs and across the yard towards Ariella.

"Are you the Baroness of Leduryon?" the woman asked in an accusing way.

Her voice had a kind of huskiness that would have been attractive to some. The duchess was a few years older than her, but Ariella would never have been able to tell by her looks. Her face was all feminine softness. Her dark, liquid eyes looked large and sensuous even in anger, which seemed to be her current state.

"Yes, I am," Ariella replied in a level tone, "Whom do I have the honor of addressing?"

The woman smirked. She was about to play her trump card, not knowing that Ariella had already guessed her name.

"I am Edoline, Duchess of Ichon, betrothed to the crown prince Demetrius."

"It is kind of you to come and introduce yourself," Ariella replied politely, "when I have not officially been summoned to the court."

"Not at all, I just happened to be passing through," Edoline pronounced, biting her lip probably at the disappointment she felt in Ariella's lack of reaction. "Do you always use a great sword?"

"Yes, I usually favor it," Ariella replied, a smile playing on her lips. She had not expected the conversation to shift so suddenly to weaponry.

"I personally prefer a simple war sword, like your instructor has over there," she pointed to Jaquelle, who was resting in the shade below the balconies. "May I?"

Jaquelle threw her sword across the sandy expanse of the yard, and Edoline snatched it from the air with a confident hand. She twirled it around, performing some impressive feats of dexterity that would be mostly useless in battle. Ariella did not wish to be intimidated by this demonstration of strength, but she was. She could see that at this point the duchess was bursting with strength and energy, while her own arms ached from the simple drills she had done.

"This is a very fine blade," she said with surprise. "Shall we have a bout?"

Ariella grinned. She was exhausted, but she would not say no to such an opportunity to take stock of her rival. She realized now that even though Demetrius may have told her the truth about his regard for Edoline, that she was nothing more than a childhood friend to him, it seemed that the duchess was a little more ardent in her feelings.

Ariella went to pick up her sword and saluted her

opponent.

"We're not wearing armour," Edoline remarked lightly. "That is a little foolish. I suppose Demetrius would be upset if I accidentally ran you through…"

Ariella could not form a response, too stunned by the implied threat.

Edoline attacked, leaving no time for words. Her technique was flashy, filled with predictable little tricks. Ariella found she could easily deflect the first onslaught. Though her opponent's blade whistled through the air with the speed of its movement, it created little more than noise. Ariella then took a couple of steps back, creating a brief pause. Now she knew what to say.

"You love him," she declared, looking in the other woman's eyes.

Edoline lunged with renewed fury. But again, she was far too easy to foil. Ariella supressed a triumphant chuckle, though upon reflection she wished she had been wrong about that particular point. Demetrius had always downplayed his relationship with Edoline, but the woman's determination to fight her rival told a different story. Ariella stood her ground this time, and tentatively advanced, trying to break through Edoline's defences.

"You love him too," the duchess responded, panting with effort, or maybe with fury.

"What does it matter?" Ariella said, thrusting forward with the point of her sword, "You are the one he is to marry."

Ariella felt that she was winning, and not only the fencing match. She advanced steadily, trying different tactics to keep the duchess occupied.

"That's exactly what I want you to understand," Edoline said through gritted teeth, "This is a marriage forged as an alliance between our states many years ago, and it will not be broken."

"Then you have nothing to worry about," Ariella retorted.

Her sword was doing its own work now. Her body was one with her weapon, and she knew just when to parry or when to step aside and counterattack.

She nearly scored a hit, when suddenly her tired right arm shook with too much tension, allowing Edoline to seize upon that small advantage immediately and slip past her guard. In the next instant, Ariella was tripped, and she fell hard on her back. Breaking some of the impact with her arms, she left herself wide open.

She looked up to see Edoline's sword uncomfortably close to her throat.

Ariella was overcome with the absurdity of the situation: here they were fighting a senseless battle whose outcome meant nothing. She burst out laughing, completely infuriating the duchess.

"This is not a game," Edoline spat out.

"Isn't it, though?" Ariella replied. She knew better than anyone that it was not a game, but she simply wanted to irk her opponent as much as humanly possible.

Edoline finally collected herself. She stepped away from her vanquished foe.

"Thank you, good woman," she said, throwing the sword in Jaquelle's direction.

The blade arced through the air, falling short of where Jaquelle sat, but with expert speed the warrior woman sprang up and caught it by the hilt. Ariella was grateful to her for this little feat of strength and dexterity, as catching that weighty sword would not have been the easiest thing. At least one of them did not fail. Jaquelle said nothing but gave Edoline a look that signified an utter lack of diffidence.

Ariella painfully rose to her feet as the sound of Edoline's footsteps died away. She came over to sit beside Jaquelle.

"Another inglorious passage of arms," Ariella remarked.

"You know as well as I that you could beat her easily when you're in full form," Jaquelle grumbled. "But the duchess is right about one thing: she is to marry the Prince Demetrius. You must not give yourself high hopes in that regard."

"She is no duchess but a vain cockatiel," Ariella replied irritably.

"Your retorts are about as good as your swordplay today."

Ariella could not believe that Jaquelle held no hope of her marrying Demetrius. After all, Jaquelle had been one of the people who convinced her to seek Demetrius' help when they were besieged. But Ariella did not wish to bring up the past. Nothing she said would make a difference. The ultimate decision belonged to the prince himself. In the meantime, she needed to regain the full use of her arms.

"Well, I believe I've had enough rest," Ariella groaned as she stood up. "Let us continue, and I pray you, Jaquelle, show me no mercy."

"I had no intention of showing mercy," Jaquelle assured her.

"Good," Ariella replied, lifting her sword into a high guard, "I need to break this losing streak."

A few hours later, having recovered from the practice bout, Ariella headed away from the castle and into Argentz, which beckoned with its spirited clamor, its enticing food smells, and its convoluted streets. This was the first day in her recovery that she felt she could walk longer distances. Enough time had been wasted resting; she needed to see how her warriors were adjusting to their new quarters and to talk with her captain of the guard about future plans. Most of these involved revenge and taking her castle back.

She took a glance at the palace which loomed behind her as she left its gates. The proud towers of white and brown brick, the red roofs, the ornate windows and majestic domes. It was his home, where he had grown up, but to Ariella it held a menacing air, too grandiose to be welcoming. She was glad to leave its opulent facade behind and explore the city on her first outing since she had arrived here.

Emelote would be waiting for her at a tavern called The Kindly Tinker. They had been sending messages back and forth via the glider that Demetrius had lent her to communicate with her people during her recovery.

She found the tavern after a bit of meandering down tiny,

crooked streets. Inside, it was dark and cozy. She spotted Emelote at once by her long, straight, blonde hair hanging down like an icy cliffside among all the dark-haired Sylcadians. The glider, a small, furry creature, sat on Emelote's shoulder, nibbling on a bean.

"I see two of our troops here," Ariella said jokingly, "but where are the others?"

"My lady," Emelote stood up briefly and bowed. "I had hoped to bring a few of our people with me, but they're most of them gone."

Only now did Ariella notice Emelote's grave expression.

"What do you mean gone?" she asked in a tense whisper as she took the seat opposite. "Dead?"

Emelote shook her head.

"Then where in the Blessed Realms are they?"

"You see, my lady, they grew restless."

"It has only been two weeks... no, three weeks? Not more than three." Ariella had begun to lose track of time during her recovery.

"Yes, three weeks it has been. And although our quarters here cannot be faulted, and we lack for nothing, it is not in our people's spirit to be hangers-on, living a life of idleness. Most of them have left to seek other work, hire their swords out in neighboring provinces."

"This is turning into quite a day," Ariella said.

"I am sorry, I tried to stop them."

"It's not your fault. I'm glad at least you have stayed. How many are left with us?"

"There's Kyra, Tycheon and his sisters, Selene, a few others... well, no more than eight altogether."

The glider, having finished its bean, chittered and jumped onto the table, where Ariella petted it absently.

"I'll have to count you as one of our warriors after all," she said to the creature.

"Do not despair, my lady," Emelote said in her earnest way, "When the time comes to take our land back, they will return to fight by your side, I know they will."

"I thank you for your loyalty," Ariella said, "Your heart is so true that you might have more trust in the others than they deserve. But truly, I don't blame them for leaving. I have no legitimate claim on their loyalty after losing my castle and my lands."

A barmaid came by asking them if they wanted drinks, but while Emelote asked for a beer, Ariella ordered only water and the same bean stew Emelote was having despite needing a drink very badly after hearing this news. She had barely touched wine or any other liquor since she lost her castle. Now, she had Ancarette to thank for keeping her sober; it was the best way to regain fighting shape, not wasting a single day on carousing, or recovering from it, a day that could otherwise be spent training.

"It will take another week at least to get my full strength back. Jaquelle demolished me today at training."

"I will wait as long as it takes, my lady."

"I may have to hold you to that," Ariella said with a crooked smile.

"But even if we did have all our warriors with us," Emelote said, "It wouldn't be enough to take back the castle, and especially not if you wish to..." her voice dropped to a whisper, "do more than that."

Ariella knew what she was hinting at, taking back not only her castle, but also the entire kingdom. They had only spoken of it in subtle whispers because after the attempt on her life in Chaldea, there could be good reason to believe that Queen Esclairmonde's reach, her spies or assassins, extended to other cities too.

"I've thought of that," Ariella replied. "We'll need funds, and definitely more warriors. I've been thinking about the borderlands."

"The borderlands?"

They had both fought there in a few skirmishes to repel the invading Koroi tribes. Ariella almost missed the place, a no-man's-land between Dezearre and the wild plains where the Koroi roamed and more often than not fought amongst each other, too busy these days to make any serious attempts to invade Dezearre. It had been three years ago, but she could still recall the sweet smell of burning wood at their encampments, the atrocious screams of battle, the terrible yet beautiful silence afterwards beneath the desert sky. She also remembered how populated these regions were, despite her expectations to the contrary. Smugglers, merchants, mercenaries, prostitutes and thieves all found ample opportunities there to ply their trades.

"There must be more than a few desperate characters there willing to join the fight," Ariella suggested. "Though perhaps too desperate... I'm not sure if I like the thought of hiring mercenaries."

"I don't trust the folk in that region," Emelote said, "Mostly cutthroats without honor."

"Maybe they're just the sort of people we need."

"Why?"

Ariella lowered her voice, "Honorable people might not wish to rebel against their queen."

Despite the disheartening news and despite the exhaustion and ache in her legs Ariella rallied as she trudged back to the palace. It felt good to be able to see the city, to walk long distances again, and she would only get stronger.

Jaquelle, on the other hand, was not in high spirits, had not been since they arrived here. The reason for Jaquelle's general discontent was clear. Ariella was reminded of it as soon as she strolled into their luxurious quarters decorated with the finest silks and arrayed with the softest settees and beds among which Jaquelle looked distinctly out of place with her sober, dark clothing and her austere, disciplined air.

She sang a sad song, one of those ancient songs whose words were a mystery, while stitching a piece of hideously brown material that looked a good match for her usual attire. Skilled in both combat and healing, Jaquelle also turned her hand to most other types of work, anything to keep herself busy.

"You've been invited to a festive dinner," she told Ariella, barely glancing up from her needle and thread.

"Oh, by who?"

"The king and queen, of course. It's in honor of Demetrius' return."

"I might as well show up, since they had to cancel the last one on account of me."

"I wouldn't," Jaquelle muttered.

"Well, I know you wouldn't."

"Keeping a low profile has been good, so far, even though that duchess is now sniffing about. Have you thought about what role you're going to play at this event? The temptress, the 'scarlet woman'? If so, there's a perfect dress for it waiting in your chamber."

"Really?"

A flutter of excitement coursed through her whole body as she went into the next room to verify this report.

Laid out on her bed in all its red glory was a dress the likes of which she had never seen. It was simply amazing. The boldness of its color drew the eye, while the cut of its design radiated grace and elegance even while it sprawled on the bed, unfilled by a human body.

"Where did this come from?" Ariella queried.

"Sent by his princeliness himself, of course," Jaquelle replied. "Does he ever stop and think before he does something?"

Ariella grinned. "No, usually not. But I've never had such a beautiful dress in all my life."

"And if you take my advice, you won't wear it."

"But I don't have any other dress to wear."

"You shouldn't attend this dinner at all."

"How can I not? The king and queen wish to see me."

"They can come and see you here if they want to see you so badly."

"Ha! Well, I want to see them."

"Like a mouse wants to see a cat. Very well then, go, since I can't stop you."

"I will," Ariella said, "I need to let everyone know that I'm here, and I'm here to stay."

CHAPTER 2

The hall was decorated with mosaics in the old empire style. Images of flowers and mythical beasts built into the walls with amazing precision distracted Demetrius from the delegation that had just arrived, mostly older men and women in long robes.

"Your Highness..." a servant whispered in a tone of warning.

Demetrius had made yet another error, bowing to all the magistrates who entered the hall, when in fact they were supposed to bow to him. Now they stared at him and muttered to each other, perplexed.

"A lifetime of servitude isn't easily erased," he said loudly to all the people assembled, not one to ignore his own mistakes. "Perhaps next time you can all bow to me twice to make up for it. Only joking, of course."

This earned only some minor chuckles. He was losing his touch.

Although he knew perfectly well he was the prince of the land, feeling it in his heart was another matter altogether. He sat down at the head of the long table.

The day seemed to go on forever in endless royal duties. Today they were discussing how the laws of the land would change if they were to ally with the Duchy of Ichon. Demetrius carried on with the discussion without trying to suggest that the wedding was anything but imminent. He would have to talk about it with his parents first; they were the ones who made the arrangement, and to break it without their knowledge would be unforgiveable.

When the session ended, he hurried from the room, eager to breathe some fresh air in the garden, where he had yet another meeting, this one more of a pleasant kind. Edoline was waiting for him, and this would be the first time the two of them met alone, though no doubt his parents had a hand in this too. They had made sure he and Edoline were never alone together in the first days since his return. They wanted him to ease back into life at the palace before such an important and sensitive meeting could take place. His best friend. The girl of his childhood dreams.

He saw her silhouette framed by the arch of the pavilion; she was dressed all in black, standing against the background of the most beautiful flowers.

She opened her arms, and he could not resist giving in to her heartfelt embrace.

"Your parents keep you busy," she remarked.

He shrugged. "Perhaps it's for the best. I don't feel completely at home yet, but maybe these meetings with the magistrates will make me forget I had ever left. That council chamber, it had seemed much bigger in the old days. Everything seems different..."

"Do I seem different?" she asked, toying with a strand of her hair.

"Yes and no. You're all grown up now. In my imprisonment, I pictured you just as I'd last seen you, when you were fifteen years old. It was my memories of you that sustained me, Edoline, kept me from losing my mind. But as I grew older, it seemed wrong to think of you in that way. You had always been like a sister and a friend to me, and in my mind, you were a young girl..."

She seemed nervous, afraid of what he might say next, so

she changed the subject.

"Have you seen your other friends?"

There were a few young men of noble rank he had been friends with, and he tried his best to spend time with them, though he found their company somewhat tedious. It was not their fault; they lived lives of carefree leisure, and had never experienced what he had suffered.

"You're the only friend I need, Edoline," he said.

A warm smile spread across her face, lighting up her eyes.

"That's what I like to hear. And soon we shall be married, as soon as you're more settled. We have missed so much time together."

He hated to bring this up now, but there was little choice. The more he delayed, the more painful it would be for her later.

"The wedding... I wanted to talk to you about that, Edoline."

Frown lines creased her forehead. She could probably tell from his tone that this boded ill.

Just as he opened his mouth to go on, who but his royal mother should stride up to the pavilion followed by the king himself. Two pages accompanied them.

His mother was on his trail like a swifthound, preventing him from having any reasonable amount of time alone with Edoline. She must have sensed his hesitation about the wedding, though he had not spoken about it yet.

"All is ready for the feast," the queen said, "Come, my dears, we must get the two of you dressed as well."

"Welcome home, Your Highness!"

"Thank you. You are most kind."

Demetrius smiled at another couple of guests who approached the royal table, then heaved an exhausted sigh as they retreated. The usually sweet and nutty muckpitts and the fragrant tortoise roots were like ash in his mouth. The clamor of the guests around him sounded rather like the cawing of crows than joyous voices raised in celebration of his return. Children ran about the hall, ruining their finery by play-fighting, crawling and slithering in the large space in the middle of the hall, and all he could think about was how soon their innocence would be replaced by sordid adulthood.

He may as well have been acting the role of the melancholy Prince Baconius whom he had portrayed in Vidor's theater. But the feast, after all, was in his honor. He tried his best to smile at the courtiers who approached the royal table to congratulate him on his newfound freedom from slavery, but in his heart he did not believe he was ever free.

"Your pretense of good cheer may fool most of our guests, Demetrius, but it will not fool me," the queen said more loudly than was necessary.

His mother's directness came as no great shock to Demetrius. Fortunately, his father, King Gaufridus sat between him and his mother, providing the cushion of intercession in their constant disagreements.

"For heaven's sakes," Gaufridus stepped in, "leave the boy alone, Larissana. You cannot force him to feel happy."

"Put on a better pretense then," Larissana suggested.

"Mother, I have left my brief acting career behind," Demetrius rolled his eyes in exasperation. He thought she would now scold him for being brash, but her expression softened.

"We have no choice," she said, "It is part of a monarch's duty to be an actor."

"In that case, dear mother, I will procure a jester's cap for you so that you may entertain us all."

"I am not about to put an end to this feast," the queen continued, ignoring his remark, "We have already had to cancel once thanks to your gallivanting. This is it. Enjoy it and let the people see you grateful for their attention."

"I will try," Demetrius agreed in sardonic tones, "even if by 'gallivanting' you mean I came to the aid of the lady who helped me regain my freedom."

He felt a stranger in this throng of courtiers. And what had he truly done to deserve such celebration? Saved his own hide, that was all.

On his other side, Edoline, sporting the colorful puffy sleeves that seemed to have taken over fashion while he had been away, was flirting with a young baron in a silly attempt to make her fiancé jealous. All he wanted was to see Ariella, and all he could think about was what was taking her so long.

It was not the custom in Sylcadia to announce the names of new arrivals at official parties, and so when Ariella entered the hall, she walked up to the royal table to make her own introduction. This did not mean her entrance went unnoticed. Whispered comments and curious gazes followed her. She walked through the main entranceway past two long tables that lined the walls, all the way to the third long table of royals.

She wore a red dress, but not just any shade of red. It was the most vivid, bold red that could be seen in the entire dining hall, and she wore it well. The bodice clung faithfully to her slim waist, and the sleeves outlined her lean, muscular arms with a dashing flare at the wrist. The skirt swung alluringly with her swift stride.

Demetrius wondered whether everyone suspected that he had that dress sent over to her, that he had chosen it himself. He scolded himself for the perverse desire for them to know that this was his woman.

He had not seen her in days. His parents had made sure of that by heaping royal duties on him since his return from Dezearre. There were courts to preside over, decrees to formulate, and council sessions to sit through. He was relieved to see that Ariella was regaining her health and vigor. Her face was no longer as pale as it had been during her recovery from the wound. Her walk had never been graceful, but it was strong and confident.

"Your Majesties," she said, "It is an honor to be here. I am Ariella, Baroness of Leduryon."

"At last," the queen pronounced, "we meet the lady who caused our son to ride off for days, abandoning his royal duties, and this when we had just got him back after thirteen years of absence."

Demetrius glared at his mother. But Ariella did not flinch at the not-so-thinly veiled jab.

"Maybe he preferred my company," Ariella replied, boldly meeting the queen's eye.

The royal princes and princesses, his aunts and uncles, as well as a few dukes and duchesses who were seated within earshot gasped at such audacity. They may have known that Ariella had arrived here because of a quarrel with one queen, but no one could have the gall to speak to their Queen Larissana in such a manner.

But the queen was unperturbed.

"You may find me more difficult to charm," she said.

"We are grateful to you," the king assured Ariella. "This feast is but a small token of our affection for you, Baroness."

Ariella bowed and walked off to take her seat.

"Though we would be much more grateful if she were removed soon to another province," Larissana whispered as soon as Ariella had gone far enough away. "This is too much, having her at court."

Demetrius felt his heart sink like a dead weight as he settled back in his chair. His mother saw Ariella merely as a source of embarrassment, or maybe even an impediment to his marriage.

His fiancée, Duchess Edoline, who sat on his right, tried to look amused, but he could tell by the way she was fiddling with her food that Ariella's presence was unsettling to her too.

Meanwhile, Ariella found a seat at one of the tables beside Lady Daphne, the biggest gossip in the kingdom. Daphne's buxom beauty contrasted Ariella's strong and lean physique. The two women's personalities differed as much as their looks did, and so he supposed they would either hate each other or become instant friends.

"Her being here does not bother me," Edoline said as casually as she could.

"I don't see why it should," Demetrius replied rather curtly.

"She is a fragile woman in need of protection," Edoline continued, "You know, we tried a passage of arms the other day, and all I can say is… I can see why she needed your help to fight her battles."

Demetrius shuddered with rage. He should have known she would not simply leave Ariella alone. There was an archness to Edoline's character that he remembered from the days of old when she had seemed to enjoy tormenting him.

"You should not have done that, Edoline," he said in a low voice deep in his throat.

For a second, the duchess looked almost frightened. But she recovered her poise and gave him a winning smile.

"I'm sorry if it upset you. It will take a little time for us to become accustomed to each other's company again, won't it? After all, we are no longer children."

She gave him a look that was meant to be seductive, but he merely found it annoying. Still, he had missed that little girl with dark ringlets of hair and bejewelled dresses that would inevitably get muddy from traipsing through forbidden boglands and forests. In those days, he would have done anything for her. Now, this woman sitting before him was almost a stranger.

It wasn't that she was not attractive, far from it. But there was no room in his heart for any woman, save Ariella. Besides, he could not understand this ardent feeling that Edoline harbored after so many years. In the old days, she had never shown him any romantic sentiment, only friendship. Of course, he had been a scrawny boy, and now he returned a full grown man, handsomely built and overall not too shabby looking.

The main course of roast pickor had been served and eaten, and now it was time for the dance.

The musicians filed into the room and began with the rousing sound of the finelle. It was a merry dance that involved leaping, spinning, and making strange figures with one's arms. Of course, Edoline expected him to dance. He took her hand and led her to the dance floor in the middle of the hall. It brought back memories of dance lessons where both he and Edoline pretended to be most unwilling, but which they enjoyed nonetheless. Now, her eyes sparkling with excitement, Edoline, his friend and companion, was before him.

Demetrius enjoyed the dance, but felt guilty for doing so. He knew Ariella would be pained to see them dancing together, a real proof of their engagement visible to all. He glanced at her talking with the gossip-mongers around her, then caught Edoline watching him, smoldering with anger.

Finally, the music came to an end, but then it was the giaronda, an even giddier dance. It did not require much skill, with everyone simply skipping or stepping in a long human chain, hands linked together. The children formed their own chain, which later wound itself into a circle in the center of the hall.

The adults were still in the midst of making their chain into a larger ring around them when Ariella was pulled into it. She was one of the people in the tail end, while Edoline was at the front. The tail of the human chain made its way around the hall, and just before it joined up with the head, the lady holding Ariella's hand fell back dizzily and had to leave the dance. Ariella was now the last person in the chain, and she had to join hands with Edoline to complete the circle. Ariella offered her hand, and Edoline clasped it with the air of someone holding a rotten vegetable. They circled round the hall, until the music mercifully came to an end.

"She's everywhere," Edoline pronounced in a fierce whisper.

It was one of those tricks of sound that carried her utterance to the farthest end of the hall in the silence that ensued after the last musical note.

Demetrius knew it was all unfair to Edoline, and that was why he needed to be open with her.

"Ariella is staying here," he said, "She is my friend, she saved me from slavery, and I will not cast her out, not even for you. I'm sorry."

Edoline's eyes filled with tears. It made him instantly regret saying anything. He hated himself for hurting her.

In the next instant, she slapped him across the face. It was not a gentle, symbolic slap either. His head whipped to the side, and his cheekbone burned.

Edoline gave him a withering look, as if to make sure that he noted how the tears gathering in her eyes did not spill. She seemed to be holding back with superhuman effort. Then she turned away and walked out of the hall.

"Welcome home," Demetrius muttered to himself.

The guests busied themselves with pretending they had seen nothing. The queen stood up from her seat, signalling the logical end of the festivities.

As everyone departed for the night, a ten-year-old boy approached. This was his cousin, Prince Marcus.

"I don't hold it against you, cousin Demetrius," the boy said, looking up at him with a serious and frank expression.

"What, being slapped?" Demetrius asked.

"That you're going to inherit the throne now," the boy said.

This curly-haired child was the next heir to the kingdom after himself, and he was the only one who dared meet his eye and talk to him after what had just happened. Demetrius was touched by his gesture.

He saw something of his former self in the boy. He used to be quite serious too in those carefree days of youth.

"But Marcus, if I produce an heir, then you may never get a chance at the throne," Demetrius stated.

"Don't worry, I will not send assassins after you," the boy assured him. "I really don't care if I become king or not. I'm happy either way."

For the first time that evening, Demetrius was surprised to feel his lips forming a genuine smile. He squeezed the boy's shoulder affectionately.

"Then you might make a good king one day," he said.

Ariella left without looking back at him. He admired her presence of mind. She was almost too good at not displaying her feelings for him in public, and he wondered if she resented him for bringing her here, in plain sight of all these festivities relating to his engagement. Ariella did not wish to be his lover in name or in deed, not while he was still engaged. To keep her isolated would be insulting to her, but to have her here observing everything was perhaps even worse. And that left him caught between two angry women; three, counting his mother.

From the dining hall he made his way into his parents' chambers. It was time to pose the question to them because things were clearly only going to deteriorate from here if they were not checked.

His father was pouring himself a glass of tortoise root spirits as Demetrius entered. He remembered the way his father would do this every night, and Demetrius imagined he had always done so, even in the last thirteen years, all that time he had missed. His father looked ever handsome and majestic, though with much more grey in his luxurious black hair than Demetrius remembered from the old days.

His mother's looks had suffered more over the years, frown lines marring her perfectly oval face.

"Ah, you've come to say goodnight?" King Gaufridus asked.

His father's voice at times held a tremulous note that had never been there before.

"Yes, but there is something else..."

Several servants were fussing over his mother as she sat before her mirror. They had removed her face paint and hair ornaments, but she still wore her festive clothes. In this mid-stage, she looked like a fraud, a common woman thrust into a queen's robe. Of course, nothing could be further from the truth.

"Please leave us," she said to the servants, and they all filed out of the room.

Demetrius watched them with sympathy. Only a month ago, he had been in their place: wearing clothes that others had chosen for him, disappearing into the shadows when he was not wanted. But now he somewhat envied them too.

Larissana did not turn from her mirror, but Demetrius could see her face reflected in it. At least his father was facing him, looking eager for his news.

Demetrius began, "I have come to ask you an important question."

"I know what you are going to ask," his mother interrupted wearily.

"Mother, how could you know?"

"I can see the way you look at that lady from Dezearre."

"Ariella," Demetrius corrected.

"You rode like a madman to rescue her," his father added with a wry smile, "I think your mother and I know what that means. And we are happy that Ariella is safe here with us."

"But you know as well as I that she cannot stay here long, and she could certainly never become queen of Sylcadia. The people would never accept it. Edoline would never accept it."

Demetrius felt all the blood drain away from his face. He had not expected his question to be predicted and dismissed so casually.

"Besides," his Larissana continued, "You must give Edoline some time to work her charms on you again. Do you remember how you used to chase after her?"

The king chuckled. "There was a time when you would do anything for her, and she knew it too, the little minx."

Demetrius recalled all too well how he would risk life and limb to steal a giant cherry from the royal gardens to be rewarded with a small, lopsided smile, and once, only that one time, a kiss on the cheek. He still remembered that kiss. He had been twelve years old then.

"Father, what do you think? Could I not break the engagement?" Demetrius asked in desperation. He knew his father usually deferred to his mother in all important questions. Somehow he did not imagine this would ever change.

"Maybe it wouldn't be so bad," the king uttered to his surprise, "for the boy to marry whom he wants."

"Gaufridus, of all the foolish things!" the queen exclaimed.

"I don't want my son to be unhappy in marriage," the king replied, "And I don't want Edoline to be unhappy either. Maybe she could marry Marcus?"

"Oh nonsense!" the queen cried. "Marcus is still a child, while Edoline is almost past her time for marriage. If something isn't done soon, she will burst like an overripe flamefruit."

"Mother, how can you not understand that so many years have passed since I was a boy smitten with Edoline?"

The queen finally turned away from the mirror. She stood up from her chair and came towards Demetrius and put her soft hand on his cheek in a rare gesture of affection. "Of course I understand, my son. I know your life has not been easy. But through these many years here without you, we suffered too. Edoline mourned your absence. She wore black all these many years, and she prayed every day for your return."

"I never deserved such devotion," Demetrius said. "How was I to know she would suddenly come to love me?"

"We do not know what's in another's heart," his mother said softly.

"I pray you, at least postpone the wedding," Demetrius pleaded. "I am not ready for this."

"The date is not yet set," Larissana said. Her tone and her look now lost that motherly warmth, but she was still standing so near him and looking intently at him. "We will not rush into it. But Demetrius, I know you would not fail in your duty to your people. Breaking the engagement would mean losing the entire Duchy of Ichon and weakening our kingdom, it may even mean war. I know the kind of man you are. You would never allow this to happen."

Demetrius returned to his room. Each night he made a supplication to the goddess of fate, looking up at the flickering star. He guessed it was she who had brought Ariella into his life. But each night she denied his prayers. He felt it. All she granted was a fitful, nightmarish sleep.

CHAPTER 3

"You are much distracted, Ariella," Lady Daphne teased.

As she walked down the gravelled paths of the royal gardens Ariella had been gazing at the marvellous red flowers whose petals were shaped like butterfly wings. She had been reluctant to have Daphne as a companion, but the lady's chatter was after all not too disagreeable, sometimes even pleasant.

Ariella envied her lackadaisical existence. In Dezearre, both men and women were trained in weaponry, even if they had another calling, so that the entire population could stand strong in case of barbarian raids. Here in Sylcadia, there was no such custom. There were quite a few men and women who had never picked up a sword or a lance. Daphne was one of them. She did not seem to have any occupation at all, in fact.

The butterfly plant attracted real butterflies that alighted on the blossoms, sending the slender stalk dancing and the pollen spilling as wings fluttered in a flurry of color. Ariella's thoughts were too heavy to be lifted by butterfly wings.

"I wish I could be distracted," Ariella sighed. "These gardens have many sights that could distract the mind."

One of these was the sight of two men fondling each other on a park bench. It was not considered proper for people of the same sex to display affection in public in many parts of the Northern Coast, but here such rules were nonexistent. Ariella felt slightly aroused and intrigued. She had never seen two men kissing before, and she decided it was foolish to outlaw such practices. Daphne waved to the couple, and they greeted her. She seemed to know everybody.

The two women walked through a lofty greenhouse filled with innumerable plants. Sheltered from the winter chill, many of them sported flowers and fruits.

"You are brooding on Prince Demetrius, no doubt," Daphne said. "Perhaps you didn't notice the way he looked at you during the banquet. He was brooding too. His pouting mien is quite an attractive sight, so I won't be the one to complain."

Ariella had never confessed her feelings for Demetrius to anyone here, and she did not like how easily Daphne had guessed them. Not wishing to be dishonest, however, she neither confirmed nor denied such feelings when Daphne ventured to talk about them.

"I wonder what reason he has to brood," Ariella said vaguely.

"Oh come, dear lady, now you are simply teasing me," Daphne giggled. "Everyone knows the reason. He is to be married off soon. Just when he has regained his freedom, he must lose it again. And obviously he is not marrying for love."

"How does everyone know this?" Ariella asked, doing her best to appear disinterested.

"It's inevitable," Daphne shrugged. "News travels quickly in the royal palace."

"And you are one of its bearers?" Ariella queried.

She had already guessed that Lady Daphne was quite the gossip monger.

They left the greenhouse, and both shivered in the humid air of the wintry garden. Here, most of the trees still had their leaves, thanks to Sylcadia's mild climate, but few fruits or flowers could be seen.

"Indeed, I sometimes think of myself as a bearer of news,"

Daphne agreed complacently, "but it doesn't harm anyone. Ariella, I want to help you. In fact, there is some information you should know, and you may not like it, but I feel that I must tell you about it."

Ariella decided there was nothing for it but to take the bait. "What is it?" she asked.

"There is talk… people, not I, but other people, are talking about you. Nobody knows exactly, but some say…"

"What?" Ariella prompted impatiently, though she feared she already knew the answer.

"Some say you're the prince's mistress."

Ariella raised one eyebrow. "And what do you believe?"

"I don't know anything about it," Daphne protested innocently, "and you're silent on the subject, but I respect that."

"You have a strange way of respecting it," Ariella declared. She had not meant to sound quite so harsh, and she waited for Daphne to take offense. Just what she needed, another enemy.

"I'm sorry if my curiosity gets the better of me sometimes," Daphne said as meekly as ever, "But I'd like us to be friends. I truly say this only with your welfare in mind, to warn you of the envious courtiers that surround you."

"And why do you seek to be friends with someone who is the object of so much rumor and speculation, someone who has no rightful place here?"

"Because I was like you once," Daphne replied, toying with the ruffles of her dress. "I mean not exactly in your place but…"

They stepped onto a small bridge and leaned on the stone railing. Below, water lilies lay serenely open to the grey skies.

"What do you mean?" Ariella asked as she observed the gently flowing water.

"I have an illegitimate child," Daphne confessed, "When it happened, I didn't know whether I would ever have a place at court again. Everyone looked at me as though I was worthless, an embarrassment to the royal court. Luckily, all has turned out well. My son remains here with me. He is educated alongside the royal children and the scions of noble families."

At this moment Ariella saw Demetrius walking purposefully towards them down the garden path. Her heart beat louder against her ribcage, and she was lost for words, with nothing to say about Daphne's story, though she was not unmoved by it.

"I want us to be friends too," she finally said, just as Demetrius stepped onto the bridge and greeted them.

"Well, I must be off," Daphne murmured. "I wish you good day, Your Highness."

Obviously she had formed her own opinion about Ariella's relationship with the crown prince.

"Shall we walk?" Demetrius asked, offering her his arm.

Ariella threaded her hand through it, and they strolled down from the bridge, into the shade of piper trees whose long, reed-like leaves whispered and sang in the breeze.

When passing courtiers looked at them, Demetrius offered them good day, in a tone that implied for them to mind their own business.

"Your mother hates me, there's a fine start," Ariella blurted out.

"She doesn't hate you. She simply wishes you didn't exist… and I strongly disagree with her."

Ariella merely scoffed. "Officially, you're probably not allowed to disagree with her."

"Believe me, I know how hard this must be, contending with my mother," Demetrius said, "she can be quite impossible. But no matter what happens, I will never side with her against you."

"She will never agree to our union," Ariella stated.

She settled down onto a stone bench decorated with the images of gods and animals.

Demetrius was silent, standing beside her and looking through the branches and leaves of the beautiful garden. For a while he stood still. His masculine but refined features tensed in a slight frown, and only his hair moved in the breeze.

"Then we must run away together," he suddenly said. "No more kingdoms and palaces and royal duties."

"You would leave your kingdom?" Ariella asked, "Leave your parents now that you are finally reunited after this long separation? And Edoline... I think you do love her in a way."

"Edoline is my friend," he admitted, "and we do love each other in a way. But she is more like my sister."

"She went after me like a firebrand burning with jealousy. A fine sister indeed!"

"I may have given her too many signs of my affection when I was young. I'm sorry I didn't tell you the whole truth. I did love her in my boyish way. We have always been so close, and if I were to leave her behind, a part of me would die. But I'm willing to never see her again in order to be with you."

"I do understand," Ariella said, although jealousy pierced her heart to hear him speak of his feelings for Edoline. "But what about your kingdom?"

"I have given enough for this kingdom," Demetrius said bleakly, sinking down on the bench beside her. "So many years as a slave, a hostage ensuring peace between our kingdoms. I have sacrificed enough."

"Is there no middle ground, then?" Ariella asked, "No way that you can be with me and yet fulfill your duty?"

"I've been going over it in my mind, but there is nothing I can think of, short of asking Edoline herself to disband the engagement. But her parents are dead, so it is only up to her. I fear what she might do, however. She's vain, unpredictable, and volatile. She hasn't changed much since our childhood. There is one other thing... my mother thinks that you cannot stay at court. She has suggested that I allot some land for you and a castle, your own domain. You could stay there until everything is sorted out."

"I hate to say it, but perhaps I agree with your mother," Ariella pronounced at length, "I feel like I'm constantly watched here, always on my guard. I await some sort of attack, but it never comes. And when it does come, I fear it will be too devastating, for I am not standing on solid ground and can't defend myself."

Demetrius clasped her hand. "Ariella, you're describing a

nightmare. This is not what I wanted at all when I brought you here. I'm sorry I have let this drag on, but I wanted you to recover your strength first. We need a better plan. In a week, Castle Reimfred will be ready for your arrival. It is part of my lands, but I have never stayed there, and the castle has fallen into disrepair. I have already ordered my people to make it ready for you. You will be a baroness with your own stronghold once again, and you'll be safe there. Meanwhile, I will make one final effort to break this engagement. If it doesn't work, I will come for you and we'll go wherever we wish."

As much as Ariella was disturbed by the courtly life, the thought of being separated from Demetrius, even for a short time, repelled her even more. However, it seemed like a wise course of action.

"It is a good idea," she said

"Good, then Castle Reimfred is yours. It will give you some ground to stand on."

"Thank you, my prince," Ariella said.

"Ariella, please don't address me in that way," he remonstrated. "Call me anything you like, call me a scoundrel and a filthy son of a bitch but do not talk to me as a subject to a prince."

"But if I am to rule one of your domains, then I would be one of your subjects," she reasoned. The last thing she wanted was to be merely his subject, but she could see a future where the wait to resolve the situation dragged on interminably until that was all she was. "Maybe that wouldn't be so bad after all. Here, I'm just the butt of all gossip."

"If I should ever find out who is spreading this gossip," Demetrius growled, "I will give them something to remember."

"It matters not," she said, though his anger on her behalf sparked a sudden desire. His blue eyes flashing like lightning, he was like a fierce god, "Courtiers who are bored need something to talk about."

They reached a more secluded part of the garden.

Wandering among the trees, they left the path, and now they could safely talk without being observed. Demetrius stopped walking and turned to face her.

She could not resist it any longer. The desire to hold him in her arms was too strong, and she yielded to it, her heart pounding with fear and excitement. Demetrius returned the embrace with tremulous feeling. The pressure of his arms felt wonderful after these many days apart.

"I love you," she whispered, shutting out all the other things she wanted to say, the doubts and the reproaches.

In response, his lips consuming hers left no doubt as to his feeling. She forgot about the possibility of being watched. The kiss, the only one they shared in weeks, burned away any doubts or hesitation. She held him tighter as her lips and tongue responded in kind, but he pulled away, looking pained.

"We could be seen here."

"I know," she said, not begrudging him the sudden ending of the kiss. It could have only led to more, and the garden was definitely no place for it.

"Soon..." he said, "we shall resume, when you'll be mine by right."

The next day passed in the usual routine. Ariella trained once again in the courtyard, and Jaquelle attacked her with even more vigor than before.

"Your strength is returning," Jaquelle remarked as they sat down on the steps for a small rest.

"At least everything hurts less," Ariella shrugged.

It was true; her muscles no longer protested at being used to their full capacity. Yet her former strength was yet to be regained, and she could not feel the Zaliati powers like she had before. If she was supposed to be a warrior of legend, that day seemed very far in the future.

"You have spoken with Prince Demetrius, haven't you?" Jaquelle asked.

"How do you know?"

"Don't look so stunned," Jaquelle said with a grin, "I would never spy on you. I just had the feeling that you were invigorated by something more than merely recovery from a wound."

Ariella breathed out slowly. "So, you didn't see us meet in the garden?"

"No," Jaquelle said in a more serious tone, "but I'm sure that sooner or later someone will."

Ariella did not like where this was going. "What are you saying, Jaquelle?"

"I remember when you told me how he had first got himself captured. Getting carried away in the heat of battle... it seems foresight is not his strong suit. That is what has placed you in this awkward situation."

"That much is true," Ariella agreed, "Demetrius does not excel at making plans. Maybe he was naive to think that this could be easily arranged, but—"

"There is no but. This needs to stop. We need to leave this place."

"I know that," Ariella cried, "by all the gods, don't you think I know that?"

She had gone over her plans hundreds of times in her mind, wondering whether she should let Jaquelle in on the secret she shared with Demetrius. But something told her not to confide in the older woman. Somehow, she could not see Jaquelle approving such an impetuous plan as running off with the prince of the realm. Besides, there was the small sliver of a chance that they wouldn't have to elope.

Jaquelle stared at her disapprovingly, a familiar sight. She did not often scold her young charge but waited for her to calm down in her own time.

"I'm sorry, Jaquelle," Ariella finally said, "It is just so frustrating, being here. And the way I feel about him... well, I suppose you've guessed by now."

"All I care about is protecting you," Jaquelle replied, "I understand that you and Demetrius are drawn to each other, and that is why your situation is so dangerous. Your feelings are too strong, and when you cannot control them, that's when you lose, in battles, and in life."

"I don't believe that," Ariella said.

"To win a sword fight, you must be fully in command of your senses. Your intellect must be as keen as your blade. Even now, you are angry with me for sticking my nose into your business," Jaquelle continued.

"You're not far off the mark," Ariella replied. "But we love each other—"

"Love is not enough," Jaquelle said.

Something in her tone made Ariella believe that Jaquelle had once experienced love after all.

"I'll risk your displeasure to tell you the truth," Jaquelle continued, "You are now attached to this man, but there was once a time when you believed one man was about as good as another. You were free to act as you pleased. I didn't exactly approve of your wasting your time in the company of men who cared nothing about you, but now... I think you're even more unhappy than you were then. Now, I see you confined here, almost like a prisoner."

"That's not true. I could leave at any time. We could all leave."

"And yet we will not leave until this matter with Demetrius is resolved one way or another. You won't take a step without him, will you?"

"Demetrius is different from other men I've known," Ariella insisted. "You don't know him."

Jaquelle shook her head ruefully. "You sound so naïve."

Ariella thought perhaps Jaquelle was right, but then she realized how unfair it was to be thus criticized simply for being in love.

"That's enough!" Ariella cried.

She did not care how ridiculous it looked; she threw down her sword and stormed off. There was no one she could confide in, Ariella thought as she climbed the staircase up to her chamber. No one, that is, except Demetrius, and he was hardly ever by her side.

That night, she could not sleep. The bed felt as uncomfortable as a rocky crag. It was around midnight as she struggled to find a restful position that she heard voices outside her chamber. A man's, humble and soft, and Jaquelle's, cold and displeased. Only a single door separated her chamber from Jaquelle's, but the apartments were placed in such a way that anyone wishing to enter Ariella's abode had to pass through Jaquelle's chamber first.

The voices continued their discussion, and Ariella sprang out of bed. She was through the door in an instant, wearing only her silk bedroom slippers and a simple knee-length nightgown.

In the next room, she saw one of Demetrius' servants, a young man dressed in the prince's colours of blue and scarlet, trying to address an indomitable Jaquelle.

"You may not, do you hear me," Jaquelle scolded, "you may not enter here and disturb the baroness at this hour of night."

"Jaquelle, let him speak," Ariella commanded.

"I am sorry to wake you at this late hour," the servant said, a grave look on his face.

"What is it?" Ariella asked.

"Prince Demetrius wishes to see you."

She felt a sense of foreboding. On the other hand, there was a flood of relief in knowing that he would finally end the torture of their separation. The need for his touch was like a constant ache, in both her body and spirit.

"You are not meant to be at his beck and call," Jaquelle cried. "This is outrageous! You're a guest here, not some courtesan."

"Jaquelle, we don't know why he has called for me."

"You won't tell us why, will you?" Jaquelle glared at the messenger.

He bowed humbly. "Alas, I don't know. But His Highness seems in a state of distress."

"Sure, if that's what you want to call it," Jaquelle growled.

"I must go if he needs me," Ariella said softly, more to

herself than anyone. She did not care whether Jaquelle agreed or not. The memory of snowy sky flashed before her, and the cold autumn field where she lay wounded when Demetrius came to her aid. She would not refuse to come to his.

"You can't go," Jaquelle insisted, "You said yourself you didn't want this."

Ariella stepped back into her chamber, where she put on a silk bedroom robe and cinched it with a belt.

"Lead on," she said to the servant.

They walked through dark and silent passages. It seemed everyone was asleep except a couple of servants hurrying on some late-night errand. The eerie quiet increased Ariella's nervousness. As the servant opened the door and motioned for her to enter the room, she was short of breath.

Once inside, she knew there was reason to worry.

Demetrius sat on the floor, leaning back against a large bed with extensively rumpled sheets. Ariella guessed, or hoped, that it was not a wild orgy that had laid waste to the bed, but the tossing and turning of someone like herself, unable to sleep. He was wearing nothing but a long, half-unbuttoned white shirt.

Beside the bed on the floor stood a half-empty bottle of wine and the stump of candle, so low it was almost extinguished. The shadows beneath his eyes had deepened so that he looked not only more exhausted and sleep-deprived than he had been the day before, but even slightly mad.

He registered her presence with a drowsy motion of his eyes, then continued staring off into space. The servant left at once, closing the door behind him.

"You can trust Orpheus," Demetrius said in a flat voice, "he would never tell anyone you were here."

"What happened?" Ariella asked sternly. She was so worried that it made her quite angry with him.

"I'm sorry I asked you to come here," he said, looking at her at last, "but you are the only one who could understand. No one here can…"

"What? Understand what?" she asked impatiently.

"I have had almost no sleep in three nights," he said softly, "I fear I'm going mad."

Ariella came towards the bed and sat down on the floor beside him. She laid a hand on his shoulder. A distant memory stirred within her, when she had been racked with a similar misery.

"I think I know what it is," she said gently, "I felt much the same when I returned to Leduryon from my first campaign on the borderlands. After so many days of war, danger, and hunger... suddenly, you are home, and safe, but you begin to feel all the fear that you had held back. I remember I wandered the halls of my castle in confusion, and I cried for no reason. I had no appetite, and I couldn't sleep."

She could tell he was listening, clinging to her every word as his gaze caressed her face from beneath swollen eyelids.

"We had quite a journey escaping from Chaldea, you and I," she continued, "It's only now, when you are free to take a breath and have time to reflect, that you truly suffer."

"I knew you would understand," he said, "but that is only a part of it. The other part, well, it is much too horrible."

He took a gulp from the bottle and offered it to her, but she waved it away. She had sometimes drunk, even to excess, before she had lost her castle.

"I can see you want to tell me what it is," Ariella argued. "There is something you have been silent about for some time."

"No, just not yet," he begged, "I can't bear to lose you now."

"Lose me?"

"If I tell you, you may despise me. After all, I despise myself for what I've done."

"What nonsense is this?" Ariella cried, her anger returning, "I'm sure you have no good reason to despise yourself. If you just tell me what happened, I can assure you of that, and then you can get some sleep."

"You say that now," he replied, his voice low but certain, "You're so trusting of me in your heart, but your heart betrays you."

He stood up abruptly and walked over to the window, resting his head on his arm and leaning against the glass.

"Maybe it's your heart that betrays you," Ariella suggested.

"Each night, I'm haunted by nightmares," he said without turning around, "I lie awake or I stare out this window looking over this domain, which shall be mine. I am the crown prince, am I not? Everyone bows before me. They flatter me, and they congratulate me on my miraculous escape, on my freedom."

Ariella came closer to him, and he spun around, his face distorted with anguish.

"I'm no longer a prince," he shouted, "but a miserable slave! Chaldea has made me what I am. I feel like a stranger here. I don't deserve all this pomp and ceremony, this glory and this wealth. I don't deserve you."

Ariella took hold of his shoulders and held him tightly, willing him to steady his nerves.

"Demetrius, what is it?" she asked. "Tell me. Do not torment me any longer."

"I shall tell you soon," he said with a sigh, "Soon, I will have the courage. Do you remember what the elf king said to me? He said my battle is yet to be fought, and how right he was. I hope I don't lose my sanity like poor Mara."

"I won't let you," Ariella said resolutely.

As soon as she said it, she doubted herself. After all, she had not been able to save Mara, the unfortunate thief who was already half mad when she encountered the elves in the Ringing Woods.

"Oh gods, I will need a drink!" she exclaimed. "But a stronger one than this…"

She walked across the room to a low table that had a number of bottles on it.

"Koroi wildgrass whiskey?" she said. "Is this real?"

"I doubt it, but a good enough imitation."

Ariella took a swig from the bottle and grimaced at the burning of the herb-flavored drink. As she set it down, another object caught her attention.

"What's this?" she began teasingly, but grew more serious when she saw his panicked look.

A many-tailed whip lay on the table, half-concealed by the assortment of bottles.

Demetrius was at her side in an instant. He snatched the whip from her, and Ariella gasped at the sight of him holding it, fear and desire mingling within her.

CHAPTER 4

Even in his ragged state, Demetrius managed to look more alluring than ever. His hair obscured half his face, blue eyes glowing behind its dark waves. His shirt, mostly unbuttoned, revealed his muscular chest. But it was not his savage strength that stood out, but his vulnerability as he held the implement of pain.

"I'm sorry," he said, "I forgot to put it away. You didn't need to see this."

For a moment she suspected him of leaving it out on purpose, but he seemed so dazed and distracted that he could well have been telling the truth about forgetting to put it away.

"Is this... does this have something to do with your former slavery?" she asked. "Did someone do this to you? Do you use this on your servants?"

He chuckled. "That's a lot of questions... but do you really think I would use this on my servants?"

Of course, she should have known he would not be the kind of man to abuse his servants.

"Well, then... how do you use it?"

For the first time since she had known him, he seemed at a loss for words. Did that mean he would finally confess some of his secrets? Was he choosing the best way to tell her? He hesitated.

At length he said, "I haven't used it yet... But yes, some have struck me with an implement much like this during my slavery."

Ariella had tried to restrain her curiosity and not to pry into his past, but now the words came tumbling out and she couldn't stop them.

"Was it the women you entertained?" she asked, "Or men? Was it Prince Theodos? Who? Did they do this against your will?"

"No," he said, "in answer to the last question. It was not done against my will, though other things were. The flogging, I didn't mind. I even liked it. It helped me to release some... feelings."

She huffed impatiently, wanting to know the answers to the other questions.

But he could be stubbornly secretive when he wanted to be. Well, there were always more questions to ask.

"Why do you like it?"

"It's hard to explain," he said, turning away, "Sometimes I think I don't know myself... But there is some sort of pleasure in it. A dark and depraved pleasure... Sometimes, I think of you, and I wish..."

"You mean, you want me to do that... to you?" she asked uncertainly.

"Yes, but that's not why I asked you to come," he said, putting the flogger into a hidden niche behind an innocent painting of a landscape. "I only wanted to see you, to talk to you."

"Maybe..." she could not believe she was saying this, "maybe if I did this, it would help you sleep."

"No," he said firmly. "I know you're not ready. Once my engagement is off, then we can do such things."

Ariella couldn't help herself. It was like someone else was opening her mouth and putting these words in it. Her desire for him was just too strong.

"Let me try," she said. "Maybe the release you seek will help you feel better."

She knew where this might lead, and maybe that was why she kept insisting in spite of herself. The thought of doing this violent ritual made her anxious, but she wanted to help him, or maybe what she wanted more than anything at this moment was simply to touch him, even if it was going to be done indirectly through an implement of cruelty.

"Do not fear, it won't cause any serious damage," Demetrius assured her. "The tails are broad and soft, not like a whip that cuts."

Ariella felt the leathery thongs that formed the tails, nine in all. To test it, she lightly whipped her own left arm. It didn't hurt at all. She flicked the handle harder and felt the sting.

More than anything at that moment she longed to hold him, to shower him with tender kisses. But that was not what he needed, or at least not what he thought he needed.

She picked up the whiskey bottle and drank long and deep.

Meanwhile, Demetrius took off his shirt, revealing that beautiful, smooth skin she yearned to touch... and that he was wearing absolutely nothing on underneath. He went to the secret compartment and took out a coil of thin rope.

"Would you care to tie me up?" he asked, "Otherwise I might escape and then who knows what I might do to you."

The look her gave her suddenly took her breath away. There was no going back now.

She tied him tightly to the bed posts, as if that would stop any temptation, and she looked over her knots with satisfaction.

She gave his bottom a light smack with the flogger.

"Is this also fair game?" she asked.

"It is, if you want it," he replied.

The tails of the flogger trailed up the sleek muscles of his legs to the tight curve of his behind and up his powerful back. It had been two months since she had last seen him unclothed, and it seemed too long. She did not touch him now, tantalizing herself with his closeness. Instead, she slowly swept the ends of the whip up his legs, then up and down his back.

"You're driving me mad already."

"I haven't even started," she said innocently. "Are you ready?"

"Oh yes," he said, that husky tone creeping into his voice.

The flogger thwacked across his back. Demetrius did not wince.

"You can hit harder than that," he teased. "Is this the arm that conquered the Koroi hordes?"

"Are you sure?"

"Trust me," Demetrius said, "I can take it. Can't you think of something for which you'd like to punish me?"

She could not. She was not angry with him. She knew that things were beyond his control, and that whatever suffering she had incurred here was not his doing.

Another stroke of the flogger, a crisper sound this time.

On the other hand... she could now take it out on him.

She liked the solid feel of the smooth wooden handle and the satisfying smack of the leather thongs on his back.

"Harder?" she asked.

Demetrius turned his head to look up at her. The madly burning passion in his eyes held a dangerous glint, though she knew not what they burned for. Punishment? Atonement? Or simply the satisfaction of some urge, incomprehensible even to him.

"Harder," he agreed.

This time, his broad back winced as the flogger struck.

"Yes, just like that," he said.

Ariella kept up the intensity, even though he winced now at each stroke, and she didn't like to see him pained. But there was definitely something arousing about his powerful body being subjugated to her. The warmth in her limbs was slowly causing her to sweat. The exercise of swinging the whip, together with her arousal made the bedchamber seem suddenly too hot.

She longed to throw away the flogger and satisfy her passions, but at the same time, the rhythm of her own strokes drew her into the action, and she would have been hard pressed to stop. Demetrius had been her slave before, and now he seemed so again, willingly. The feeling of power over his perfect, masculine body made her thighs clench with desire.

His back began to look raw, covered with criss-crossing lines, but he showed no signs of wanting to stop. He shifted his hips, a movement that Ariella caught, strongly suspecting it was to accommodate his erection.

"Yes," he groaned deeply, "Harder!"

Ariella used her full strength now. He grunted with every blow, which lashed his already reddened skin.

His eyes were closed in ecstasy or anguish. The sound of his panting mixed with the cracks of the whip.

Ariella realized that he may never ask her to stop or to ease up. His pain was too much for her. She raised the flogger for the last time, but did not strike. It dropped to the floor, its clatter accentuating the sudden silence.

"Why did you stop?"

"Because you've had enough."

"I know when I've had enough."

"Well, so do I," she said. "Tell me what happened in Chaldea! What did they do to you? Was it Prince Theodos?"

He propped himself up on his forearms, but the hair falling over his face concealed his expression.

"I think you might have guessed it already."

The starkness of what he said was frightening. She thought of one of the worst things that a human could do to another without killing him. If the answer was that simple, then Ariella was frightened of hearing it. But still, she needed to know.

No longer in control of herself, all she knew was that her hip touched down on the bed, and then she was leaning down, holding Demetrius' panting body in her arms. It felt like trying to calm a wild horse. The great heaving mass of his torso seemed menacing, but it held no threat for her, especially since she knew how much gentleness he had shown before.

Her eyes closed, there was only his racing heartbeat, even faster than hers.

"Untie me," he breathed.

Ariella hesitated.

"Perhaps I should just leave you as you are," she said with a chuckle that concealed her uneasiness. She was fairly sure of what would happen if she untied him. It was just a small step from being rumored as the royal mistress to actually becoming one.

"Untie me, Ariella," he pleaded, "I need to hold you."

The husky urgency in his voice was irresistible. It opened up an aching emptiness inside her. Before her mind could protest or formulate another plan, her fingers were working at the rope.

This was what she feared would happen, what she wanted to happen. As soon as Demetrius was free, he turned fluidly, embracing her with effortless grace.

There was no more disagreement in her mind. It felt so right to hold him tightly, to yield to his caresses and let herself be held in his strong arms.

The touch of his lips brought everything back. Not that she had forgotten how warm, how alluring they were. But to kiss him again, it broke the thin veneer of isolation that had prevailed these last few weeks, the barrier that had seemed so impassable. Yet here they were, clasping each other strongly to reclaim possession.

Ariella laughed giddily. She was with her lover again. There were no more restrictions, at least not in that moment. He smiled, seeming to understand the reason for her laughter. He didn't smile so openly very often, but when he did, he became irresistible.

She seized both his wrists and pinned them to the bed just at the level of his shoulders. He seemed pleased with that and did not try to resist.

She had almost forgotten the way his scent, his closeness made her dizzy. Just the mere thought of what they were about to do pierced her belly with lust too intense to stand.

Touching him again was so new and so familiar. She had forgotten the sounds he made, soft groans of pleasure that sometimes gave way to deeper growls as her hand grazed his thigh in a seductive sweep around, but not quite touching his manhood.

Her hands reacquainted themselves with his long, silky hair, his broad chest, and the rough stubble on his jaw. She stroked them ceaselessly, but it was never enough. She wanted to merge with his body.

In one fluid motion, she took off her nightdress, and his hands needed very little invitation to roam her naked skin.

He rose up on his elbows, mouth reaching ravenously for her breasts. At first she pulled back to tease, but then let him fill his gorgeous mouth with one while his hand cupped the other with a light touch. Now it was his turn to tease with his tongue's tender nudges.

Even as she was about to request harder pressure he squeezed her breasts with both hands. Her heart suddenly raced, and her breath, what little of it was not swallowed up in passionate kisses, quickened even more.

"Your breasts are so beautiful," he said.

"Is that why you want to squish them to a pulp?"

He laughed. "You like it."

"Maybe I do," she conceded.

She returned the favor by biting down on his shoulder and then his chest, the sensitive skin around his nipple.

He gasped. "By the ever-living stars, what are you doing to me?"

"I think you like it too," she said, glancing up at his face for a moment.

"Maybe... oh!" he groaned as she bit him again. "So you want to play rough, do you?"

He flipped her over and pinned her wrists like she had done to him.

"You only succeeded there because you had the element of surprise," Ariella said.

"Then you should easily escape this hold."

She twisted her hips, gaining some leverage, and then pushed her right arm against his left. Demetrius resisted, though she couldn't tell whether he was using all his strength. The resulting struggle left them hanging halfway off the edge of the bed, with neither side able to gain the upper hand.

Demetrius paused, his grin changing to a more serious expression. The combat seemed to inspire him for more passionate exertions. He gave up the fight, and brought his lips to hers.

There were still stray thoughts of caution, that she should not be here, should not be doing this, but they faded like wisps of fog in the heat of his touch.

She felt her body being pulled back fully onto the bed. As she lay across it, his kisses lingered on her neck before he sampled almost every part of her upper body with his tongue. Her breasts tingled at his attentive strokes, then even her shoulders and her arms met with adoration from his eager tongue and lips. His mouth traveled down to her navel, and by the time his breath wafted across her thighs, she was trembling and ready to come...

All it took was his lips placed lightly on the wetness of her center.

Just like the first night they met, when Demetrius was the willing slave, he submitted to all her desires, and she knew he found enjoyment in fulfilling hers. She had never been shy in bed, and she now did what she wanted. After recovering from the first amazing orgasm, she began savoring the taste of his skin, the hardness of his manhood as she rubbed against it before taking it in her hand and slowly inching her way down to engulf him.

There was nothing that could compare to that feeling when she possessed him, and was possessed by him. It was amazing to see his perfect face reflecting all the pleasure from the things she was doing to him.

She tried to hold on to that feeling, grinding against him slowly, but her desire was pushing her to complete the journey. She leaned forward, stroking her center against his hot skin. The stimulation, both inside and on her clitoris was so strong that she soon lost all control and let the peak of pleasure sweep down through her thighs and up to the very tips of her hair, the strength of the orgasm escaping from her lips in a fierce cry.

She collapsed onto his broad chest, resting her head on the pillow, her cheek against his. In a few moments, he let her catch her breath, and then gently turned her onto her back, he began to move with a slow rhythm. This time, she did not try to fight as she lay back and enjoyed each slow, sensual dip and rise of his body. She had a perfect view of his arms flexing around her, his upper body rocking back and forth as her hands caressed its taut muscles.

He took his time, leaning down to kiss her, his hand adding to the intense sensation by stroking her nipples, his tongue licking along the hollow of her ear, making her gasp.

She expected it to take a long time to climax at this slow pace of lovemaking, but that gentle sensation of his tongue on the delicate skin of her ear pushed her over the edge with an equally slow-building invasion of ecstasy in every part of her being.

Demetrius got up to light a new candle, for the one he had at the foot of the bed had long since gone out. In its light, he looked at her admiringly. It was the first time he noticed the scar on her chest. Jaquelle's healing hands had made it almost imperceptible, but the memento of the duel with Ancarette was still there, glowing white in the light of the candle.

He leaned towards it with a look of concentration, and for a moment Ariella thought he was just looking at it closely, but then he kissed the scar.

She had not words to thank him for doing that. She simply returned the kiss, merging her lips with his in a sweet intoxication of delight.

CHAPTER 5

Soon they had no need of the candle as the room was lit by the pre-dawn twilight. Demetrius took a tray of fruit from his nightstand and put it on the bed.

"Shall I feed you the fruit like the dissolute bastard that I am?" he asked.

"Why not?" she said. "I've been quite dissolute myself. Eating fruit in bed will be just the proper ending to this event."

Pleasantly tired and hungry, she enjoyed the grapes, so ripe they fizzed, and the flamefruit, sweet and unbelievably juicy, with just a hint of spice, especially when he fed them to her.

"I'm sorry that I called for you like this in the middle of the night," he said. "I should have known this would happen. You wanted to avoid becoming entangled with me, and I failed you."

"No," she replied, "It was foolish of me to think we could go on being apart. I realize now that we're meant to be this close to each other... or at opposite reaches of the earth. But there is no middle ground."

"Not for us," he agreed. "Especially not after Prince Baconius."

Ariella laughed. "I wish I could forget about that damned play. It was so embarrassing."

"That's not true, I remember you liking it."

"I liked that you were in it," she allowed.

Demetrius frowned. "If you keep heaping praise upon me, I might not be able to say what needs to be said."

Ariella's body stiffened next to him. "You mean, about your past? You will tell me what troubles you?"

"Yes," he replied. "I better tell you now or I'll lose my nerve."

"So, who was it that did the flogging to you the first time? Was it a lady?"

"Yes, a lady from the southern reaches of the empire."

"Was she beautiful?"

"Yes," he admitted, relishing the fond memory, "It doesn't make you jealous, does it?"

"A little, but that's in the past. And it's not worth being upset over for you either. It's only a game... or is there something more that troubles you?"

He had to talk about it now, or he would never bring it up again.

She was silent, waiting for him to go on.

"But first, you must swear on the thing you hold most sacred... Swear that you will not try to take revenge on anyone for what I suffered."

"Was it Theodos?" she asked immediately.

"Swear," he insisted.

"I swear," she said, "that I will not take revenge."

"So..." Demetrius sighed. "It is something that happened in my days of slavery. The first few years were, in fact, not bad at all. King Acheron treated me with all the respect due to my rank. I lived in luxury, and there were few things not permitted to me.

"But, soon after I turned eighteen, my body completed its growth into full manhood, and I acquired this masculine form which you see before you now, and which is devilishly striking, if I may say so. I attracted women's gazes, but I also attracted the attention of the prince himself."

"He was attracted to you?" Ariella asked.

"Yes. I often caught him devouring me with his eyes. It

made me shiver, though I had no idea what it portended. But soon enough, I understood. It was an obsession. He waited for me in dark corners, he knocked at my door late in the evenings, he whispered to me during meal times. One day, he asked if I would join him in his chambers."

"You're saying he was in love with you?" Ariella asked, sitting up in bed.

"I don't know if he ever loved anyone," Demetrius replied bleakly, "but maybe something like it. He liked becoming close with people and tormenting them."

"But you didn't love him…" Ariella said uneasily. "Did you?"

Demetrius hesitated, wondering just how shocked she would be by the truth. If only it had been that, if only he had loved another man, who happened to be Prince Theodos. That would have been nothing. But he had resolved to tell the full story.

"I have never loved any man in that way," he said firmly.

"Yes, go on," she breathed.

"So, it grieved me when he forced his attentions on me."

There. He had said it. He had said it too flippantly, but at least he had managed to confess it to one single person, the one person who mattered most to him.

Now that it was out of the way, the rest of the words tumbled from his lips easily enough.

"I made it clear to him one day. I tried to tell him gently, and he seemed to understand… but later that night, after dinner, I felt more drunk than I should have been. There must have been something in my wine. I felt dizzy, and I was near collapsing when the prince and some of his guards carried me to his chamber. What happened next, I don't remember… at least I thought I didn't remember. When I awoke, my entire body was in pain, covered in bruises and scratches, and I knew he had violated me, though I didn't know whether I had been conscious during this time or not. Often, he taunted me about it. He knew I couldn't remember. But that's not all."

"What more?" she asked, gazing at him with what looked

like pity, though she was trying not to make it too obvious.

"Please don't look at me like that," he implored, "I don't deserve it."

"Tell me," she said.

"Fortunately, one day the king found out about his son's little diversions. Ironically, it was his taunting me that gave him away and made the king ask questions, and I don't know how but he sensed the truth. He sensed I had not been there of my own free will, and ever after that he made sure I was better protected. I was safe for many years, until King Acheron died and I ran away with you. The worst part is that ever since I came home, I started to remember. Was it the beast we encountered in the elf forest that awoke this demon, or did coming home make me face the truth?.. but the cause doesn't matter. I see it in my dreams, everything that he did to me when I was in my weakened, drugged state. Maybe it was the potion he had put in my drink that caused me to forget, or maybe I had pushed that horrible scene from my mind. But it did happen, and I had been awake then. I pleaded with him. It was pathetic. But he had his guards chain me to the wall, and so when I was helpless, he did everything he wanted to me. Well, not everything, for I did try to bite and scratch him as much as I could, the only meager defences I had. I wish I could just forget it ever happened, but every night forces me to relive it all in my nightmares. So you see, this is why I can't sleep."

Ariella didn't move. Her face was stiff as if someone had struck her, and he hated that he had done this to her.

He could tell by her ragged breaths that she fought hard to stem the tide of tears, but still a disobedient droplet coursed down her cheek.

"What have you done?" she whispered forlornly.

"I know," he pronounced, "it was contemptible. But it is only fair that you know the truth about me. I wanted to end my life, but I was too cowardly even for that."

"Stop it!" she exclaimed, "Where you have done wrong is in torturing yourself all these years. None of it was your fault!

Besides, the coward's way would have been to end your own life, but you fought to survive. You did what you had to do to save yourself. You were strong where many others would have perished."

Demetrius saw a glimmer of hope in her words. Maybe she did not despise him after all.

He smiled in spite of himself. "You will say anything to absolve me."

"Because you deserve absolution."

"If only I could have it. But ever since that day when Theodos first took me by force, I feel as if I was no longer myself but a lesser being."

"You are not a lesser being!" she cried hotly. "Oh, I'll kill him! I will seek him out and kill him!"

"You promised," he reminded her.

"I don't have to kill him myself," she muttered, "But maybe pay an assassin to do it."

Demetrius grinned. "I think that would not be quite true to the spirit of the oath."

"I see now why you fought him back in Chaldea. We shouldn't have run. You were right. We should have fought and killed him."

She strode over to the window and leaned her head against it like a prisoner with no hope of escape.

Demetrius came over to her and tried to calm her, holding her tightly.

"I know how you feel. I've dreamed of it many times, but now I have begun to think that even killing him wouldn't help."

He studied her face closely. "I'm sorry," he said, "I should not have burdened you with this knowledge."

Ariella stared blankly for a moment, but then her eyes lit up.

"I may know a way to help you," she said, "but it involves Jaquelle."

"That gloomy old crow? I think not."

"Why do you say that?" Ariella asked, drawing her

eyebrows together.

"She would sooner skewer me than look in my direction," Demetrius replied. "I have the feeling that she understands everything that goes on between us, and she hates me."

"Well... that may be true," Ariella admitted, "but she has the healing powers that could help you. I quarrelled with her today, so it may take some begging, but I think she can heal you."

"This is no wound," Demetrius argued.

"And Jaquelle is no ordinary healer. She could spot a wound that is not in the body."

"She did wonders with your sword wound," Demetrius said. "What can she do with me?"

"Remember when I told you that I didn't feel like myself after the war on the borderlands? Jaquelle helped me then. She said that a piece of my soul had become lost and misdirected, that it needed to rejoin the rest."

"A fine tale indeed," Demetrius scoffed, "but I don't believe anyone can mend souls. She probably just soothed you with her words."

"All right, I understand if you disbelieve, but soon you'll see," Ariella said with a smile.

"She's like a mother to you," Demetrius said, "then we shall break both our mothers' hearts if we run away together."

"I don't want to think about that," Ariella murmured.

She stood there for a while in silence, holding him.

"I must go," she said, "to preserve my reputation for a little while before completely destroying it by running off with you."

"Are you angry with me for asking you to come to me?" Demetrius asked.

She shook her head. "I could have said no, but I think we both needed to do this."

After she left, Demetrius was finally able to sleep. It was a fitful, light sort of sleep, but better than none at all.

He woke up, groggy, but filled with a new sense of purpose. He could not let Ariella languish alone without a friend. Plucking a single grape from the tray as a nominal breakfast, he strode towards the remote southeast wing of the castle.

There, he found her. Her movements precise and swift, she attacked invisible opponents and parried phantom blades. He admired her discipline, training as ever on this day despite all that had happened in the night, and despite the fact that her trainer, Jaquelle, was nowhere to be seen.

"Jaquelle is still mad at you, I take it?" he called down from the balcony.

Ariella looked up and greeted him with a beaming smile.

"Come down here!" she shouted.

As soon as he had reached the courtyard, she offered him a sword, which he took. Ariella wasted no time and began to tie a thick slab of leather armour to his torso.

"You must replace her," Ariella said. "I dare say you could use the exercise. You look terrible in the light of day."

"Coming from you, I will take it as a compliment," Demetrius said, saluting her with the sword.

She did not return the salute, still gazing pensively at his face. Demetrius now regretted telling her his secret, for he could see that it weighed heavily on her. Instead of taking a fighting stance, he let his arm relax.

"Ariella, let us go, let us run away now, today," he exclaimed. "It pains me to see you cloistered in this far-off wing of the castle. We'll finally be free."

But Ariella looked down and shook her head.

"I want to see you well first," she said softly.

"I am well!" he objected.

"You must promise me you will let Jaquelle work her healing magic on you. Until then, we shall not venture. It's too dangerous. I fear what this secret will do to you. Now, let us work on your swordplay," she concluded, trying to sound more cheerful.

They commenced fighting. Neither was very aggressive, but Ariella was slightly more inclined to attack. She was trying to advance on him carefully.

"You're being quite gentle," he remarked.

"Only because you look tired today," she said.

"Me, tired?"

Demetrius knew she was right, but he tried to rally some energy and resist her assault. He could just manage to stand his ground, but the sword felt heavy in his hand.

"I will find Jaquelle this very day," Ariella warned, "Be ready to receive her."

"Very well, if it is your wish," Demetrius replied with mock suaveness.

He knew Ariella too well. He guessed that if he goaded her into attacking more, she would. Her quickly kindling excitement got the best of her, and she began to enjoy the fight.

She attacked with unexpected rhythms, almost throwing him off balance a couple of times.

But then, all of a sudden, she stepped back and lowered her sword as a sign to pause.

"What is it?" he asked.

"I simply thought, this one time, I don't want to win or lose. If I win, it means your defeat, and if I lose... well, I just cannot live through another loss right now."

"Your duel with Ancarette, it bothers you much that you lost?" he stated more than asked.

"How can it not?" she replied. "Sometimes I think..."

"What do you think?"

She turned her face away, ashamed of any weakness as usual. Not so much of showing emotion, she had never been ashamed of that, but of what had happened on that day.

"I think I should have died there. It was a fair duel, and I was defeated."

"The circumstances that brought you to that field, they were unfair. You should never have had to fight that battle, neighbor against neighbor. And she didn't have the right to kill you."

He spoke with a certainty that surprised even himself. The matter of honor was a tricky one, but there was always a right and wrong aspect to everything that overrode the simple rules of combat.

"Take some of the same advice you gave me," he continued, "and don't judge yourself so harshly."

She nodded acceptance.

"Besides," Demetrius added, "honor can only be restored if you're alive. The dead can do nothing in this world."

"Not unless I became a ghost and haunted Ancarette into absolute misery," Ariella said with a tiny smile.

He parted from Ariella feeling in better spirits. Though he didn't want to leave her side, she urged him to go in order to avoid frustrating his mother and giving rise to further gossip.

And as he headed for the garden, plans for the future forming in his mind, the past strode boldly in, taking the beautiful shape of Edoline. How many times he had thought of her during his years of slavery, imagined returning to his best friend, and he had hoped, his future wife. But things had changed. It was not her fault. He was the one who had grown apart from this place of his childhood, while Edoline was ever the same.

Even now she smiled in that cheeky, provocative way.

"I'm not apologizing for what I did," she said without preamble.

"No need, my lady," he replied gallantly.

"Why not?" Edoline flared up, "Do you care so little about me that it matters not what I do?"

"Maybe I deserved that slap," he suggested.

"I hope not," she said menacingly. "But then again, maybe I shouldn't be surprised that you needed another woman to distract you in all those years apart."

"Edoline, I must tell you the truth—"

"No," she cut him off with a desperate look in her eyes.

Obviously, she must have guessed much of what he had to tell her.

"I do not wish to know. Whatever happened, even if you had a hundred, a thousand different women… the important thing is, you're here now, with me. Come…"

She grasped his hand, as she had done so many times in that previous life, the life of innocence and peace, pulling him deeper into the garden.

"Where are we going?"

"You'll see," she said mysteriously.

He had yearned for her company, for the sound of her laughter all through the thirteen years of his life in exile. These were the last days he would spend with her. The least he could do is give in to her wish this one time.

CHAPTER 6

Ariella had an uneasy feeling about Jaquelle. They had been in disagreement about many things lately, but they had never quarrelled as bitterly as this. The stubborn woman could not be found anywhere.

Having once again checked their chambers, Ariella strode distractedly into the center of the palace, where courtiers pretended not to stare at her. At last, a familiar face appeared, though it was not Jaquelle.

"Ah, there you are!" Daphne cried.

She was breathless, her large bosom heaving rapidly.

Although she had only spoken twice to this lady, her company was welcome, and Ariella greeted her in a friendly way.

"Shall we go for a stroll?" Daphne offered.

"What, now?" Ariella asked.

"Why not now?" Daphne said, laughing giddily.

Ariella stopped to gather her thoughts.

"I was looking for Jaquelle, but it's probably no use today. She doesn't wish to be found. You're right, I much prefer the garden to the palace."

Daphne seemed even more bubbly than usual, doing more than enough talking for the two of them.

She gabbled on about the latest fashions, something Ariella

would not have been disinterested to hear because she found the fashions of Sylcadia completely amazing, if only she could focus her mind on the present moment and not on how to talk to Jaquelle or how to plan her elopement. Would Jaquelle ever understand? Her mentor was not unattractive, she certainly did not seem unlovable, and had surely known what it was to love once, though maybe not… Ariella had never known Jaquelle to have a lover or a child of her own. She suddenly felt guilty, wondering if Jaquelle's role as her guardian prevented her from forming any other relationships.

"But then of course, you probably find those puffy sleeves ridiculous, don't you?" Daphne was saying in the meanwhile.

"I… don't mind them," Ariella forced her mind to jump into the conversation with relative ease. "I would have to try them on, I suppose."

She would have loved to have nothing more to be preoccupied about than whether this or that type of sleeve would suit her.

They wound their way up a small hill, Daphne puffing resolutely on ahead, as if resolved to reach the summit of a famous mountain. From the top, they could see much of the rest of the garden.

They could even see something Ariella instantly wanted not to see. At first she tried to imagine that the man dressed in a white shirt and grey hose was not the same one she had trained with but an hour ago, not the one whose bed she had left earlier that night, her mind reeling with troublesome thoughts, her body glowing. But there was no denying it. The sound of voices she recognized at once, Demetrius and Edoline. Loud boisterous voices, even laughter.

Never had laughter sounded so vile to her ears, as if they were laughing at her, maybe at her presumption that she could stroll into this place and take his heart, when it had belonged to Edoline all along, all these many years.

They chased each other through a copse of feeble, leafless trees for all to see, or at least for the few people who were about in the garden. Edoline's beauty shone in a long, sky-blue dress.

And just like Ariella and he had done earlier, they were sparring, but only with the fallen branches of some tree, not with swords, and Ariella hated them for it.

Not that sparring with someone always meant one had feelings for that person, but in this case... she had to wonder.

They were playing like children. Maybe he was happier with Edoline. Maybe he didn't need someone like Ariella, practically a stranger to him compared to his childhood sweetheart.

She could hear snatches of their make-believe dialogue, where Demetrius spoke the lines of Evrain, "I demand vengeance, elf queen. No one but you can help me now." And Edoline replied, "First, you'll have to prove your worth."

A sudden thought made her stop in her tracks, froze the breath inside her. Someone wanted her to see this. Surely not Daphne, who fidgeted uncomfortably under her probing gaze.

"Perhaps we should take a different path?" Daphne suggested feebly.

"Is that what you really want me to do?"

No, she was not the one behind this, though she was part of it.

Ariella instead followed the voices of her lover and his childhood sweetheart. Still engrossed in their bout, which now turned into a chase, they left the copse and entered a more wild part of the garden, a meadow that sprawled between two forested areas.

Demetrius and Edoline were now even more visible from the top of the hill, though a few trees that grew on the slope hid Ariella from their view, or at least she hoped they would, if the couple thought to look up, which they did not, too enrapt in their chase.

Ariella ran almost parallel to them along the wooded ridge. She tried to stay a little bit behind them, but could still hear their voices, while Daphne lagged even farther behind.

It was beyond her control, the desire to see what they would do when they thought they were alone. Everything about their movements roused her suspicions. Daphne followed, trying to keep up with her run.

At last Edoline stopped running and once again raised her "sword", a crooked stick. Ariella stepped a little further down the slope, trying to see. She hid behind a tree, its bark rough and cool on her hands and her cheek.

Instead of the feverish energy with which she had fought and ran earlier, Edoline now flourished her stick with deliberate slowness. Demetrius did the same, and they approached each other warily, their weapons meeting ever so gently as they performed a slow dance of fanciful attacks and parries. This looked like another game from their childhood, some secret joke they had shared for years and years, and Ariella wished those sticks were real swords that would pierce her heart instead; it would hurt less than what she was feeling now.

When she saw them moving closer together, the sticks crossed between them, she was almost not surprised by what came next.

With torturous slowness and languidness, Edoline leaned forward towards his lips. Her face passed the barrier of the crossed swords. Surely Demetrius would step back now. He wouldn't kiss her. Ariella trusted him that much.

She realized how mistaken she was. Not only did he not step back, he leaned just the slightest bit towards her.

It was not a game, at least not a childish game anymore.

Before Ariella could decide what to do, whether to storm down there and reveal herself, even though she had no real right to be angry, or to run back to her chambers, Demetrius collapsed as if the kiss had killed him.

Edoline's anguished cry reached her, and she saw the duchess catch his lifeless body, trying to cushion his fall.

"I'm sorry," an out-of-breath voice said behind her. Daphne had finally caught up. "I never would have done this, but my child… she threatened my child's future. Please forgive me."

"I don't have time for this," Ariella said as she ran towards the meadow.

Her heart pounded as she hurried down the circuitous path to where he lay. She didn't know whether it was fear for him or the desire to kill him with her own hands.

To her horror, he was still lying there, attended by the hateful duchess.

But for the first time ever, Edoline did not look at her in a hostile way.

"Please stay with him," the duchess said breathlessly, "I will call for a physician."

Before Ariella could respond, Edoline was off.

Daphne joined her now, her fine dress torn by the brambles on her way down.

"Leave me alone!" Ariella shouted.

Daphne shook her head.

"I knew something didn't seem right. Were you supposed to bring me out here to the gardens so I could witness this..." Ariella could barely choke out the words, "them kissing?"

Daphne nodded in wordless surrender.

"I'm sorry."

Ariella sensed that Daphne herself had no malicious intent.

"I'm guessing Edoline was in on the plan. She didn't seem very surprised to see me here... It's not your fault. I know exactly who planned this."

It could be none other than the queen herself. No, she couldn't blame Daphne. She did blame Demetrius. Although he was merely an unwitting actor in this performance staged for her benefit, no one had forced him to kiss that vixen.

Demetrius' hand was feverishly hot.

"Daphne, if you truly are my friend," Ariella said, "please find Jaquelle, the woman who accompanies me. Do you know what she looks like?"

"Yes, I've seen her before."

"Tell her to wait for me in our chambers. I'll do another search of the gardens, but if it fails... your help would be most welcome."

"Of course," Daphne said.

She was left alone with Demetrius, but not for long.

Edoline came running over with physicians and servants carrying a stretcher.

"Thank you," Edoline said, returning to the usual cold manner in which she addressed Ariella. "We will not need your further help."

At last, something seemed to go right on this horrible day. Jaquelle was waiting for her in their chambers. She looked up sternly from a book she was reading as Ariella entered, breathless from searching the grounds.

"That buxom lady told me you were in a panic. What on earth has happened?"

"Demetrius has fallen ill. I was looking for you because he needs your help. Also, I wanted to apologize for earlier. I lost my temper needlessly."

"Are you only apologizing because you need me?" Jaquelle asked.

She was clearly in a mood.

"No. You know I can't stand it when we fight."

"I know, and it's all right," Jaquelle replied, "I'm not angry with you, but I doubt I could help you with what you ask."

"Oh, I knew you'd be stubborn about this."

"Me, stubborn?" Jaquelle laughed. "Look at yourself, baroness."

Ariella was too exasperated, too anxious to reason with her in a logical way. She realized suddenly she was pacing the room like a caged animal and threw herself into an armchair instead.

"All you think about is him. What about us?" Jaquelle queried.

"What about us? We're fine."

"I think not. We are without a home, and we're in danger here, especially if you plan to do anything for the prince without the queen's consent. And I'm guessing both the queen and the duchess want you to stay away from him. Now that he's incapacitated, they can enforce it, too."

Ariella groaned. "You're right. If the queen and Edoline are by his side now, they won't let me anywhere near him. But I can't stand not knowing whether he's alive or dead, or how bad the illness is."

"There are hundreds of other people in this castle who can stand it perfectly well," Jaquelle replied, "You can wait for news like the rest of them."

"But I can't."

She envisioned breaking into the room, knocking out the guards if the queen went so far as to post some there, fighting Edoline again, only to see him. Of course, it was insane.

"I am finished with this conversation," Jaquelle stood up to leave the chamber, but Ariella grasped her arm.

"There must be something we can do, Jaquelle. I know you could think of something if you really wanted to help me. Why won't you help?"

"You are losing sight of who you are because of him," Jaquelle cried. "And it makes me angry."

Indeed, Ariella had never seen Jaquelle like this. The woman hardly ever raised her voice, but now she was yelling.

"I know who I am, but that's not the point. I must help him. You don't understand, Jaquelle, he has been through something terrible. All these years, it has been eating away at him. It's not a coincidence that he's ill."

"Why should that concern us? Let his physicians deal with it."

"Jaquelle, if you ever cared about me, if ever you were a friend to me, you will help him."

Jaquelle sighed, stepping away toward the window. Ariella let her think for a moment that seemed to last decades, hoping that she would have some kind of answer.

"One thing's for sure," Jaquelle said at length, "I am not going anywhere near him. The queen would have my head, and yours too if you're not careful."

"But you'll help?"

"Yes, I'll help if that's what you want. But I don't think any good will come of it."

Jaquelle rummaged in a leather satchel that held her few

belongings and took out a flat, grey stone, smoothed by ocean tides.

"I can try to see what I can see from here," she explained. "At least you will know how bad the illness is."

"Thank you," Ariella said.

She could finally draw a deep breath, though she rubbed her face nervously while Jaquelle closed her eyes, preparing to travel into her healing realm, her hands hovering over the grey stone. Ariella went into her bedchamber to give Jaquelle some room to work in.

All she could do now was wait... The tension was too much, but she sat on the bed, holding her head in her hands until at last Jaquelle opened the door. Her face was grave.

"You were right," Jaquelle admitted, "His spirit is shattered. This is the true cause of his illness. The spirit is weakened, and the body follows."

Ariella stood up, feeling at least some sort of relief that she knew the source of the illness.

"Can you help him?"

"There is a very small chance... but it might be more merciful to let him die."

"No!" Ariella cried out at once, "You're only saying that because you want me to be free of this attachment. I never thought you so selfish, Jaquelle. I remember you once tried to save a horse with two broken legs, and you didn't give up until you healed it."

"I meant what I said," Jaquelle replied levelly, "He has suffered too much, and his spirit wishes to leave. You are the one being selfish in your attempt to keep him alive."

"So you will not even try?"

"I'm not the one..." Jaquelle said mysteriously. "But if you truly want to try, you could do it."

"Me?"

"You have all the same powers that I have," Jaquelle explained, "only stronger. I was never meant to be a hero, only a guide, a mentor. My powers were given to me by the gods when I was in a desperate place, a place like the one you're in now. Only I was alone, wandering in the mountains. I had made a grave mistake, and that was why I sought redemption, and the gods heard my prayer. When I first cared for you as your nursemaid I only wanted to protect you, so I taught you how to defend yourself first of all. There would be time to teach you the healing powers later, or so I thought."

Ariella was lost for words. At last Jaquelle had revealed something of her past, even though it came out in an almost incomprehensible torrent, Ariella clung to every word. She wondered if despite wanting to seek redemption through taking care of her as a child, Jaquelle was envious of her powers. That must have been the reason why she had shared so little of the knowledge. Although it may have been true that her nurturing disposition was to protect the child she had raised, she thought she detected a bitter taint to Jaquelle's speech. But she did not want to believe this. It was not the time to think of such things.

"Do you think I could try to work the cure without entering his chamber, like you did?"

Jaquelle nodded. "If you pick it up quickly, you could try."

"Show me how to do it."

CHAPTER 7

In her mind, she fell into a strange world, watery and filled with echoing music. Everything lost its contour, and one thing blurred into another. She felt a sleepy drunkenness, as if she were slowly drifting away from her body, which still sat in Jaquelle's chamber; now she and Demetrius were somewhere else.

It was a meadow, a beautiful meadow with red and yellow flowers and a rushing stream nearby. This was a restful place, but Demetrius was walking away from her towards the sound of the rushing water.

She tried to stop him, but she could not quite walk fast enough to reach him. The meadow slowed her, as in a dream, the more effort she put in, the more she slowed down.

But Demetrius was not completely oblivious to her. He turned around, as if she had called to him. Although he seemed to try, he could not come any closer to her either.

Slowly, ever so slowly, he fell back onto the grasses of the meadow. They swayed around him, and Ariella didn't know whether they were burying him alive or protecting him.

"Someone's coming," said a voice.

A swirl of confusion descended on her, and the dizzying unsteadiness returned as she found herself once more in two place at once, vaguely recognizing that the voice was Jaquelle's, that it was warning her of danger. Her mind was drifting away from the meadow, no matter how hard she tried to stay, to find Demetrius again even though his blurred-out form was completely hidden by the clinging plants.

Her consciousness returned to the chamber where she sat on the floor, her hand still moving in circles over the smooth, grey stone. When she opened her eyes, she saw Jaquelle standing over her, looking impatient.

Ariella started as the door to the chamber burst open and Edoline marched in.

"Sorcery, I knew it!" the duchess exclaimed.

Ariella's recent emergence from the healing realm left her too dazed to react. No words formed on her lips to respond to the intrusion.

At length, she came to her senses and realized Edoline was talking impassionedly, and the general sense of the words finally became clear.

"I knew you wouldn't dare enter his chamber," Edoline was saying, "not in my presence, but instead you use this underhanded witchery? He called your name out in his delirium. I know you did this. Your jealousy turned you against him, and so you would rather see him dead than married to his rightful fiancée."

"I was trying to help him," Ariella replied, feeling drained from the magic, and too stunned to put up much of an argument.

"You're a witch!" Edoline cried.

"I'm not a witch," Ariella said wearily.

Like most of Edoline's outbursts, this was completely ridiculous. But this time, it was no laughing matter, for the duchess seemed dead serious.

"You dare to deny it even when I catch you here doing your secret magic."

Jaquelle stepped in, "Your Grace, it is a healing magic. She was trying to help cure the prince's illness, that is all."

"A fine excuse," Edoline smirked.

Just as she said it, four guards entered the small chamber.

"Seize them both!" Edoline ordered.

Ariella didn't have her sword, but she jumped to her feet, ready to put up a serious fight. Jaquelle's hand on her shoulder stopped her as the older woman shook her head. "It would be useless," she said. "We could never fight our way free from the palace."

The guards gripped their arms preventing any last hope of escape.

"To the dungeons," Edoline said.

The guards put them both in the same cell, which was both a consolation and an inconvenience as Ariella didn't want to be alone, but at the same time she was nervous about having a peeved Jaquelle to contend with.

"I'm so sorry, Jaquelle," she said, "you warned me, and I didn't listen."

"Not an unusual turn of events," Jaquelle replied curtly, sitting down on the moldy hay that was the only thing to sit on in the cell.

Ariella leaned forward against the bars, trying to discern some sort of escape route, but all she could see was dank stone walls.

"They must release us soon," she said, "Everyone will see that her accusation is madness."

"I doubt it," Jaquelle said darkly.

"But there is no evidence!"

"She saw you using the healing stone. That's evidence enough for her. I'm just sorry I couldn't snatch it from your hands, but that would have broken the spell too suddenly, which would have been dangerous for your spirit."

Ariella growled in frustration. "That foolish wench! Does she truly believe what she's accusing me of?"

Since Jaquelle maintained a bleak silence, Ariella answered her own question, "I think she does."

She started inspecting all corners of the cell, looking for loose bricks or any kind of weakness in the structure. She shook the iron bars just in case any part of them was loose.

But nothing yielded to her touch.

"It's a quality cell," Jaquelle volunteered.

Exhausted, Ariella sank down onto the hay.

"And the worst part is, I don't know if the magic worked. In that other world, I couldn't reach him... He was there, but I couldn't talk to him."

Jaquelle gave a forceful sigh of exasperation. "We might be executed for witchcraft, but all you can think about is whether you saved your precious prince."

The evening dragged on into night. Ariella fell into a shallow sleep, but woke up to the despair-inducing greyness of the cell. Jaquelle seemed to be having more success with slumber.

The more time passed, the more she realized Jaquelle's grumbling was not unfounded: all she could think about was whether Demetrius was well, alternating with endless questions about the kiss she witnessed. Did it mean he was enamored of Edoline once again? Her own fate, though it seemed to hang on a dangerous precipice, did not trouble her as much as those questions.

A couple of hours later, the guards came for them again and brought them to the throne room accompanied by the ringing of chains as they walked.

If people had stared at her before, furtively and slyly, they now did so unabashedly, for she was a criminal, her wrists bound with a heavy chain. And most of these looks were not sympathetic.

The queen, resplendent in her heavy jewels, sat on the throne beside her husband. They were equal rulers by law, but Ariella now had no doubt about who was really in power.

"You two stand accused of a serious crime: conducting evil magic that caused the crown prince's illness. Let Duchess Edoline of Ichon bring forth her accusation."

Edoline stepped forward from the throng of courtiers, her

twitching lips and clenched fists showing her utter failure in trying to look calm.

"I was walking with my betrothed in the royal gardens, not knowing that she was spying on us."

"I wasn't spying!" Ariella exclaimed.

"Silence!" said the queen, "You will be heard in your turn."

"So," Edoline continued, "we were walking, reminiscing about some of our childhood games, and then we kissed."

This revelation sent a shocked and excited murmur through the crowd.

"Yes, I kissed him for he is my betrothed, and it is my right. Then Prince Demetrius fell as if struck by a deadly illness that came on him so suddenly it couldn't have been anything natural. Then she appeared out of nowhere. I didn't put it together at the time, but she had been watching us, and she was consumed with jealousy. That is what made her put a curse on our prince."

"Did you see her cast the curse?" asked the queen.

"Yes! She was holding this stone!"

Everyone gasped, seeing the evidence in Edoline's outstretched hand.

"As far as I understand, holding a stone is not a crime in this kingdom," King Gaufridus spoke up.

"But what if the stone was—"

"It was used for healing!" Ariella interrupted. "Yes, I used magic, but it was to help him."

"She admits it!" Edoline cried. "She did use magic."

"We do not know whether the magic was used for good or ill," one of the queen's advisors said. "Perhaps that is what we need to determine."

A man in black, evidently one of the physicians, approached the throne.

"If I may speak, your majesty..."

"Of course."

"Prince Demetrius has been in a fever all through the night, a very dangerous fever. His condition is worse than before."

The queen stood up.

"My son is on his deathbed. And if they didn't cause this, if they were truly trying to help, wouldn't he be recovering now? No, I believe this magic was done with ill intent. In this extreme circumstance, I must take it upon myself to judge the matter and forgo the council's advice. I declare Ariella, Baroness of Leduryon, and Jaquelle of Leduryon to be guilty."

There was whispering all around, but mostly people seemed to approve of the verdict.

"Their punishment, if they admit their crime, is immediate exile," the queen continued, looking meaningfully at Ariella. "If they persist in denying it, then death."

There was silence all around. Ariella clenched her fists, unable to make the fateful decision. Pride and anger burned in her chest, making her unable to utter the words that would free her, albeit marring her good name. As to that, what did it matter? Her reputation was already somewhat ruined, why not have everyone believe that she was an evil sorceress?

"Shall we confess?" Jaquelle whispered, "Even if we do, they might not let us go."

"There is little choice," Ariella said.

At this moment, a collective gasp interrupted them.

Demetrius, looking pale and disheveled, but fully dressed, his sunken cheeks and weary eyes making him look somehow even more handsome than ever, stood in the doorway.

"I've heard about what you're all doing here," he said, "You accuse them of evil magic?"

"You should be in bed," said the queen, "You're ill!"

The physician who was trailing him now tried to pull on his sleeve. "Your majesty, I warned him about leaving his bed, but he wouldn't listen. Your Highness—"

"Let me be!" Demetrius cried angrily. "Listen to me, mother. No matter what happens to me, I forbid you from trying Ariella and Jaquelle. They are our guests."

"Guests who would do evil upon you?" Edoline objected.

"What evil?"

"She was doing witchcraft, I saw her."

"It was this 'witchcraft' that woke me from my helpless

state," he said. "In my feverish dreams, I saw Ariella taking me to a place of healing. Whether it was something she did, or just a dream, I came to my senses feeling much stronger."

"Perhaps then it's a different kind of witchcraft," Edoline muttered, "the kind that keeps you doting on that woman."

Demetrius turned away from her, disgust written on his face.

"Guards," he ordered, "release them."

The queen nodded her agreement, and the guards obeyed. Ariella regarded him with gratitude but wished that like the queen she could order him back to bed.

The guards opened the lock of her shackles, and she had freedom of movement in her arms. She felt like fleeing the place, for she did not fully trust that she was safe.

"Neither of them is to be harmed," Demetrius continued, "even if my illness worsens, they are not to be blamed for it, and if I die, let that be my dying wish."

He took a few steps toward Ariella, but just as he almost reached her, he collapsed. The queen let out a strangled cry, but two pairs of hands caught him immediately. Ariella looked up from his lifeless body as they held it together and met her rival's glare with a look that she tried to make impassive. She didn't want this to be about her; she simply wanted Demetrius to be safe.

Of course, Edoline would never read it that way. However, his last words must have made an impression because the queen pronounced:

"You are free to go if that is what my son wishes. I will not hold you accountable."

Then she commanded the servants to take him to his chambers, and Edoline followed them.

Ariella bowed and turned to go, though she knew she would not be welcome at his side. At least by retreating to her chambers away from everyone's accusatory whispers she would find some relief, knowing she had done everything she could to save him.

"Baroness, one moment!" an icy cold voice reached her, the

queen's voice.

Ariella turned reluctantly.

"I have been meaning to speak with you for quite some time," the queen continued. "Please come back. We must talk, one on one."

This was obviously not a request but a command.

Ariella could barely stop her hands from shaking, and she was not in good shape to confront the queen, but there didn't seem to be any choice.

Everyone else, even the guards, filed out of the hall, leaving the two of them in a space that grew suddenly vast and empty. The door clanged shut behind the last person to leave.

Ariella didn't want to be the one to speak first. The queen had no trouble beginning, however.

"You care about Demetrius," she said. "I can see that. You risked much to try to save him."

Ariella kept her silence. So the queen had never believed in the accusation of evil magic, but would have gladly had her killed for it anyway, or at least exiled.

"Now that he is on the mend, and you yourself are fully recovered from your wound, there is no need for you to be here."

Now it was surprise that kept her speechless. The queen could be outspoken, but she had never been this blunt before. Ariella never imagined this could happen. There had been a time when she thought she could get along with the obstinate woman, win her over. It was obviously not to be. The mother of the man she loved hated her. This hurt her more than anything else.

"Are you denying me your hospitality then?" she pronounced.

"Do you like it here so much that you wish to stay?" the queen countered.

Ariella feared where this conversation was going, and although she still had her pride as a noble woman, she sensed the queen had the upper hand. Everything that had led up to now had been her majesty's doing, and now she aimed the final stroke.

"You have done everything you could to make me feel welcome," Ariella replied, lashing out in desperation.

"Yes, I have," the queen agreed, ignoring the sarcasm.

"You have even staged a little play for my benefit."

"All of this has gone far enough," the queen said sternly, "You may accuse me of all manner of things: of being unwelcoming, of not being concerned about my son's feelings, even of staging a play. But there is one thing I cannot be accused of, and that is being a poor ruler. The people of this kingdom need stability. Demetrius knows that, even you know that. You have seen how much fortune war has brought your own domain. We will not have it here, not over such a matter as this. If this engagement is broken, if Edoline is rejected, she would not react with gentle grace."

"Of that much I am sure," Ariella said.

"You and she are not so different. You're both spoiled children who grew up without parents to educate you. I see that you will persist no matter the cost to anyone else. But surely you can see that it's madness. What did you plan to do, marry the prince despite my wishes? I can tell you now it's not going to happen. Run away together? Foolish. You would be captured and only embarrass yourselves further. Not to mention the chaos it would cause our kingdom even if by some small chance you were successful in making off with the prince of the realm."

Ariella wanted to storm out of the room, but the queen's cold words sank into her heart, rooting her to the spot like a magic spell. There was an iron clad logic to all of it.

"At the same time," the queen continued, "I could not see Edoline tolerating him having a mistress. And you are not the sort of woman to be a mistress. I may not know much about you, but that much I know."

Once again, Ariella could not object.

The queen said after a pause, "Spare yourself and him and all of us any further pain. Take all your people with you if you wish; if not, I will protect them within my walls and care for them as if they were my own children. But one thing is certain: you must leave."

Her throat felt so constricted she could barely speak.

"You're right, Your Majesty," she pushed the words out, "My mind has been clouded of late, but you have made everything clear to me."

She walked out of the room forgetting to bow or say anything more.

Blindsided by the queen's impeccable logic, she felt some anger, but mostly pain. She had not lied to the queen. It was not exactly that all her thoughts were very clear now, but some irresistible feeling or idea, she couldn't even tell which, was rising to the top from the whirlwind of her confusion. One thing was clear.

As soon as she was back in her chamber, alone, she spoke it out loud:

"I have had enough."

A few months ago, she never would have imagined staying in a place where she was so unwanted only for the love of a man who was engaged to another. It was all like a bad dream.

Jaquelle had been right: she was not herself. This love, if it was that, made her a pathetic shadow of her former self.

Well, no longer.

She wrote a quick note to Jaquelle. Then with quick efficiency she gathered her essential belongings. Her sword, a few warm clothes, some coins that would be accepted in all parts of the former empire.

Ariella felt no compunction about raiding the kitchens. If Queen Larissana wanted her gone, then the kingdom would be one round loaf of bread, three heads of cheese, five tortoise roots, and ten apples poorer for it. Ignoring the protesting cooks, she took what she needed and left the palace by the back gate.

After the fateful duel, the Baroness of Ancarette had taken Ariella's horse, Destiny, along with everything else that had once been part of her estate. Ariella didn't want to steal anyone's horse, and besides, a rider was more easily spotted and tracked than a humble traveler on foot. She wore her simplest cloak, which was also the warmest, red with a white fur trim.

Aside from her own castle, there was only ever one place she had lived for any decent length of time, a place she knew fairly well. It was a good place to go for someone wanting to disappear.

CHAPTER 8

King Theodos rode through the dimly lit forest, several
score of his guards behind him. Never one to linger behind the
battle lines, at least not since the fateful mistake he had made
in letting that woman escape his grasp, he led his troops
onward, disdaining any possible dangers the night could offer
him.

She had evaded him twice. Once, through his own fault
when he underestimated her, sending guards instead of moving
in for the kill himself. Then a second time, thanks to that
rebellious innkeeper. The time to make Vidor pay was long
overdue.

Night birds called stridently to warn their fellows of his
passing. As he neared the inn, he slowed his horse to a walk.
He hoped his arrival would not have been anticipated, though
he wouldn't put it past Vidor to post sentries all around his
miserable inn.

"Light your torches," he said softly to his men.

The order was passed down the ranks, and the flames were
passed from hand to hand, each torch lighting the next. They
advanced at a slow walk towards the yellow light in the inn's
windows.

A young boy sat outside. On seeing the riders approach, he
did not come forward to greet them but dashed inside. That

was probably as good a lookout as Vidor had. Perhaps he had overestimated the innkeeper, Theodos thought.

"Now," he commanded, and threw his burning torch onto the roof, setting a small conflagration.

His men followed suit. Some threw their torches high. Others shot flaming arrows at the wooden beams of the structure.

The noises coming from inside, the shouts of panic, were most amusing.

Those who foolishly rushed out the front door were picked off with arrows, all too visible in the light of the burning inn. A man in expensive clothing, a noble that Theodos thought he recognized walked out unhurriedly, about to say something, maybe to protest. He had clearly not expected to be shot down by two arrows.

The king dismounted unhurriedly. No one could possibly escape that inferno, but he wanted to make sure that Vidor would not, wanted to watch him die.

He walked past the nobleman who kneeled at the front of the building, clutching at the two arrows in his chest. He seemed to have a beseeching air as he looked up at the young king, though maybe it was just pain.

"I do not tolerate traitors," Theodos said softly, walking past him and into the burning building. "Please do me the courtesy of slowly bleeding to death."

And anyone who frequented that inn was a traitor. It was well known that the innkeeper proudly disdained the king's law and harboured criminals.

Inside, there was little to be seen or heard but the roar of the flames and running footsteps.

It seemed no one was fighting the fire. Everyone was escaping, but where to? A back door or a secret exit perhaps. He followed the sounds, speeding up his pace.

As he turned a corner, he spotted someone at the far end of the corridor who had to be Vidor. That man fit the description. He was tall, long-haired, with a bald spot, and he wore long, loose clothing.

"Hurry!" he was saying as several men and women descended into a hatch in the floor.

Theodos rushed down the corridor. The innkeeper meanwhile ushered the last person inside the tunnel, made a rude gesture at him, and promptly took the exit himself.

Theodos pursued him. Rage burned within him hotter than the flames that consumed the timbers of the building. It meant possibly cutting off his own escape because no doubt the burning inn would soon collapse, but he didn't care. There was a way to follow the traitor, and he would catch him.

Without hesitation, Theodos leapt down the hatch, nimbly descended the staircase, which, as he suspected, led to a long underground tunnel. The footsteps of his enemies echoed in the distance, but he thought he could see a shadowy figure standing calmly as if awaiting him.

"Vidor?" he cried.

He thought he could see the figure giving a slight bow.

"I'm honored by this visit, Your Highness. But you should turn back now, before it's too late."

"It is you, isn't it? No one else could be that insolent." It did not escape him that Vidor intentionally called him by the title of a prince, not a king.

"Turn back," the man called, an edge to his voice.

Theodos rushed down the passage.

Then almost at once, he sprang back. He realized why Vidor had been warning him. The innkeeper's faraway figure moved its shadowy arm, maybe pressing a lever, or even releasing a simple crank. The noise came like thunder from overhead.

Giant boulders tumbled into the passage. Theodos leapt back. It was not enough. Some kind of container or ceiling above him had come loose, and rocks hurtled down in every which direction. He ran back to the staircase, pursued by a torrent of rock.

He made it up the staircase, into an inferno of flame. There was no clear passage out. Fire all around him, dancing its way from the walls to the floor and closing in on him.

Theodos did not let this frighten him. He had become fairly adept with the magical crystal in recent days.

He tossed it into the air and let the energy swirl around him in millions of ice-blue specks. It fanned the flames into a frenzy but kept him perfectly protected within its bounds.

Timbers were collapsing all around him, but he knew it was not his destiny to die in this ordinary fire. Calmly, he walked through the flames out of the burning inn.

His men were finishing off any outlaws that had tried to escape. But it seemed Bran had been wise enough to take at least one prisoner, and what a prisoner. He looked like a god in comparison with the guards who held him and tied his hands tightly behind his back. In the light of the deranged flames, his blond hair shone like woven gold. His blue eyes seemed to beg for mercy yet they stabbed Theodos' heart with their deadly beauty.

"We never caught Vidor, Your Majesty," Lieutenant Portul reported.

"I know," Theodos said, "He's escaped into a tunnel, along with the rest of his scum. There's no way to know where the other end of that tunnel comes out... though I suspect..."

"The Ringing Woods?"

"Yes. The only place Vidor knows I can't reach. One day, the elf king will regret giving shelter to all my enemies."

"Your Majesty, this prisoner was one of Vidor's servants," Bran said stepping forward and motioning for the other guards to bring the young man. "He might know something that could help us find him."

Theodos would remember to reward his captain of the guards for not killing such a fine specimen. He approached the prisoner.

"Who are you?"

"An actor," the young man said.

The prince could well believe it. Although he must have been terrified, the prisoner did not cower. He looked graceful, even with his hands tied and held roughly as he was by the guards.

"Although..." he continued, "no longer. My stage is destroyed."

"There might be other stages," Theodos suggested.

When they returned to the palace in Chaldea a few days later, Theodos decided it was time to have a serious talk with the prisoner and had the young man summoned to his chambers.

Being an actor, he was adept at not showing fear, but the king could tell this was not the bravest man he had ever seen. A little persuasion could convince him to serve the empire's needs. Maybe there was even something else, something other than fear that hummed in the air between them.

The actor looked straight ahead, too tense perhaps even to take in the silken embellishments on the walls of the vast chamber, the luxurious furniture, and the colorful paintings.

"I trust you have no complaints. My servants treated you well?" he asked.

He had no need to, for he could see the young man had been bathed and given a comfortable silk robe similar to the one he was wearing himself.

"What's your name?"

"Xanthus."

"It suits you. A beautiful name."

Theodos circled his prisoner, with the two goals of admiring his magnificent form and intimidating him.

"I've summoned you here because I need you to perform a service for me. If you do this, I will spare you, despite your association with those traitors."

"What is the service?" Xanthus asked.

"I have no doubt Vidor will turn up again in some remote province. Maybe even sooner than I expect. I have sent spies to all corners of the empire to spot him. But you... you will be better than the usual spies. Vidor already knows and trusts you. As soon as I know where to seek him, you will rejoin him, return to his employ, and report to me on his doings."

"You wish me to spy for you? I think not. Even if I wanted to, Vidor will not trust me once he suspects I had been captured by you."

"Don't try my patience, boy. I give you a simple choice, serve me or die."

The king took his sword from where it hung on the wall, drew it from its sheath with a loud ring and placed the tip against his chest. Xanthus stood still; his breathing quickened but he did not flinch.

"You wouldn't kill me."

"You're so sure of that? I killed my father with my own hand."

"So it's true..." Xanthus said softly. "Why?"

"Why? A good question," Theodos said, withdrawing the sword from his chest, "No one has dared to ask me that before. Maybe one day I will tell you."

The young man seemed to relax a little, sensing that he was reprieved at least for a while.

"There is something else."

"I don't know what else you would want of me, Your Majesty? I'm naught but a humble actor."

"Because you are an actor, you are good at... picking up on cues."

On impulse, Theodos dropped his robe to the floor and untied his undergarment, letting it fall carelessly where it will. The prisoner before him took in a shuddering breath, but this time not in fear, definitely not in fear.

"Well, are you repulsed by what you see?" Theodos asked, glancing down at his own chiselled body.

"No, Your Majesty, I am not repulsed at all."

"Then you may stay in my chamber tonight."

Theodos lay down on top of the covers and made an inviting gesture.

"If Your Majesty wishes—"

"I do wish it," he said impatiently.

"May I not sleep on that settee there?" Xanthus asked.

Theodos urged himself to be patient. There was never quite

as much satisfaction in forcing someone to do his pleasure as in having them come to him of their free will.

"I suppose you may," he grumbled.

The prisoner settled down on the far side of the room as Theodos extinguished the lamp and lay in the warm darkness, still not using or needing his silken bedcover. He enjoyed the silent tension in the room, like the stillness before a storm.

"And yet you will join me in my bed tonight," he said at length, "I know it."

His feelings did not mislead him. He did not know how much time had passed. Half an hour? An hour? Then he heard footsteps across the room and felt warm lips against his.

Then came the soft touch of lips on his neck. Xanthus' lips kissed their way to his chest, devouring his nipple in their warm embrace. He couldn't help but groan with the sensuality of that moment. His mouth moved down to his navel, licking his smooth, flower-scented skin.

Then it was on his cock, the tongue making circular motions and stirring up the flames of desire in his entire body. He groaned louder when Xanthus took his whole length in his mouth. His hips pushed upward, and his whole body throbbed.

"You have done this before," Theodos said through ragged breath.

"Only in the theater," Xanthus freed his mouth to reply.

"Don't stop!" Theodos commanded.

Theodos stretched out in a leisurely pose, staring unseeingly at the bed's canopy in a blissful daze, while Xanthus lay on his side, facing away from him.

Theodos felt his new companion shudder. He rose up on an elbow and saw the silent tears running down his face.

"What is it?" he asked, "Don't tell me you didn't enjoy that."

Xanthus shook his head.

"You ask me to betray my friends, and I fear I will do it because I am weak."

Theodos wiped away the tears with his forefinger and thumb.

"Do not trouble yourself with such thoughts. As the king, I must be strong, but you don't have to be."

***

"Another one," someone said in a bored voice.

Ariella turned her head as she felt a pair of eyes on her.

The man that had spoken was tall and bulky, both muscle and fat outlining his imposing frame. He sat in the middle of the bar, at a slight angle from her, since she preferred to sit at a table on the less crowded side and not have her back to the rest of the drinking hall.

She decided not to speak to him. There was no point in looking for unnecessary fights. In an establishment like the Sprightly Pig fights broke out all the time. Fights over gambling, fights over unpaid debts, fights over unfaithful lovers. To her it all seemed a waste of time.

"A beautiful maiden, who thinks she's above it all..." he declared.

"What?" Ariella asked, not yet threateningly but harshly.

She didn't like to be disturbed. Since she had fled from Sylcadia, she had spoken very few words at all, only what was necessary. Silence was a blessing.

"You believe that all of this depravity and squalor that surrounds you can't touch you. It has nothing to do with you, oh no. You're only here to nurse your grief."

He spoke with the accent of a Chaldean but wore the clothing of a Koroi, as did many of the people in this region on the outskirts of the desert. After all, the roving barbarians had adapted well to the local climate. This man imitated their style with loose trousers and a long sleeveless shirt overlaid by a leather vest as well as leather armor on his legs.

"Perhaps you believe that you're able to read hearts and minds like some wizard?" Ariella asked, looking over at the stranger. "I knew someone who could do that. He could take one look at you and tell what you have done, what you feel, what you will do… but you're not the elf king."

He gave a cold chuckle. "No, hardly." His face, which seemed handsome for a moment in a rough sort of way, quickly resumed its look of bored callousness.

"What are you, then?" Ariella asked.

"A merchant."

She had come to know and understand different types of merchants that passed through the borderlands. Most of them were traders in other people's pain. Slavers, whoremongers, robbers, and purveyors of all manner of intoxicants.

Was she truly that predictable? Were there so many others like her that this dealer in human misery could easily spot her type as easily as she could spot his? She was angry at herself for even taking the time to think about it.

"You may be a powerful merchant," she said, not deigning to look at him, "and you may have some bodyguards sitting in this very room, hidden where I can't see them, but I could still slice you open before any of them can blink. Maybe I can show you your inner workings as cleverly as you've shown me mine."

"You could," the man agreed, "but you won't."

"And why not?" Ariella asked, taking another gulp of beer.

"Because even though you believe you have escaped from whatever former life you led, a life of nobility most likely, judging from your refined speech, you still have some remnants of honor left. You wouldn't kill someone merely out of spite."

"On that account, and on that account only, you are right," Ariella allowed.

"Then I advise you to be careful," the man said, "Even the slightest bit of chivalry could get you killed around here faster than carrion berry."

"Thank you for your advice," Ariella replied scornfully, "I will give it the attention it deserves."

She didn't understand what the man had wanted of her, and didn't like dwelling on it. There was probably nothing more to it than the desire to unsettle her, which probably gave him some false feeling of power.

When she was finished eating and drinking, she climbed the narrow staircase to her room. By the standards of this lodging, her chamber was bigger than most, for she didn't like a completely suffocating space, but the furniture was no more than a bed and small stand with a wash basin by the window. This suited her well.

Her new life was one of simplicity. She was satisfied with the simple food, the tasteless beer. She could have demanded higher wages, taken more dangerous assignments or sought more powerful clients, but she had no desire for the riches it would bring. Any luxuries or pleasures she could have bought with extravagant sums of money would be nothing compared to those of Demetrius' bed.

She had a few gold coins saved, but these were not enough to hire an army that could defeat Queen Esclairmonde. If she were to amass anything more, she soon would need to hire her own guards to protect the hoard, and she was not ready to make such bold moves.

In a way, she was living the way Jaquelle wanted her to live, the pure incarnation of a warrior. There were no distractions from her practice, and the occasional encounter with bandits and raiders sharpened her skill.

The next morning Ariella sat in the sunshine outside the Sprightly Pig, the inn where she rented her usual room. The day was a hot one, just like all the previous days before it. The sky looked different here from the one in her kingdom. It was lofty and cloudless, overlooking the desert plains. Nor Kemur always survived the drought thanks to being built beside a small river, although the reprobates who stumbled by seemed to live on alcohol alone. Not many people disturbed her solitude during the hot daytime hours; the town came alive at night.

Ariella would throw each of her six knives at a stout log, embedding them in the wood all in a neat row, then retrieve them and do it over again. Just as she got up to fetch them, she heard a name she realized was hers.

"Cashain!"

It was a name she now answered to. She did not reveal her real name and title to anyone in the borderlands, both out of caution for fear that either Esclairmonde or Larissana would want to finish what they started, and because she wanted to forget her former life, at least for a little while.

The thirst for revenge was always there, and even as she threw her knives, the satisfying thunk of steel into wood conjured up images of stabbing through Esclairmonde's heart and the queen looking down in shock at the torrent of blood. But she was not ready, not yet. It would take all her strength to go up against the queen, and for now, she felt empty.

She was still in a strange, slow daze ever since she had fled from Sylcadia. She had not even the interest to think of a new name for herself, so she told people to call her 'warrior' or 'guard' if they must call her something. But the folk of the borderland town Nor Kemur where she was usually based quickly found her a nickname as rumours spread of her determined loyalty to any travelers who hired her for protection. She never abandoned a companion and always saw them to their destination even in the face of some daring raids by bandits or barbarians, or sometimes both groups when they teamed up in strange alliances.

Once she was fairly well-known in Nor Kemur, they started calling her Cashain, which meant 'faithful dog' in the Koroi language, but it was an honorary if slightly mocking title, for it was a reference to the honorable knights errant of old, humble and faithful warriors who had done great deeds.

It seemed like a name given in grudging respect.

The man who called her name did not look like the kind she usually dealt with. Judging by his sun-browned skin and simple, dusty clothes, he was probably some kind of worker or farmer. More often, she was hired by merchants to protect their cartloads of wares along the dangerous road out of the barbarian lands into Dezearre, but sometimes the poorest peasants gathered enough money for her fee. Not that she charged all that much, but most people had no money at all.

The farmers usually didn't get paid in coins, and the rest of the borderland people soon lost what money they had on gambling, whoring, and drinking.

"Cashain, my name is Peiter Som. You once accompanied my cousin Ness to Dezearre."

She had not seen him around Nor Kemur. The town supported a few hundred people at the most, and Ariella had gotten to know most of their faces, so he must have come from the wild lands of the Koroi.

"You have a job for me?" she asked, pulling one of her knives out of the log.

"We'll need protection on the road. My wife Jin Lu my son Seth and me are off to join my cousin, to work on his farm."

Having collected all her knives, Ariella turned to face them. His wife looked even more bone-thin than him, exhausted by work, but unyielding in the face of her troubles.

It was a familiar story. Many people wanted to travel to Dezearre, to live in peace there without being overrun by the constantly warring tribes of the Koroi.

"How much money have you got?"

"Twenty-five old-empire Rals."

It was only half of what she usually worked for, but she didn't like to decline any paying job, and sometimes she accepted less. It was not that she needed the money very badly, having completed a few lucrative runs, but the work itself kept her instincts honed.

With the corner of her eye, she saw the boy edge away from his mother. He found a solid stick and began to lunge at an unseen opponent, uttering soft cries of triumph.

"Very well, it might do. Who else is guarding your convoy?"

"No one, Cashain."

She almost thought he was joking, but he did not seem to be.

"No one. You wish to hire no one but me. With at least five others, you might have a chance, but I can't protect you alone."

"It's all I can afford," the man replied. Unlike most men

who lacked money he did not try to pretend he didn't, nor did he look ashamed; his bony face showed determination. "And I have faith in you, Cashain."

Ariella sighed. She admired the man's courage, or maybe she could relate to his desperate need, a position she had known only too well.

The boy, despite seeming busy with his game, must have overheard them talking, and came forward, brandishing his stick.

"I'll help! I'm a good fighter."

Ariella smiled, something she hadn't done in many days, maybe weeks. "Are you? Let's see some attacks."

The boy lunged forward with a ferocious yell at an unseen enemy.

"Not bad, not bad," she said with a grin.

She handed him one of her knives.

"Here, hold it by the blade when you throw it."

"I know," said the boy.

"Think you can hit that log from fifteen paces?"

"Of course."

The boy retreated a bit from the target. With a flick of his wrist, he set the knife quivering deep in the log before anyone could blink.

"You are a warrior," Ariella said this time seriously. "All you need is a little training. What about your father? Can he fight?"

"Not as good as me," the boy stated.

"Seth is right," the father said, "I don't have the fighting spirit as much as he does, but I served in the army of one of the Koroi chieftains a few years back. I can swing a sword if need be. You wouldn't be alone."

"And your wife?"

Peiter shook his head. "She has no knowledge of fighting, and I hope she never has to."

The woman, still standing a ways back, still silent, followed the conversation but said nothing. She must either think her husband was crazy to take them on this journey or maybe she wanted this more than he did. Either way, there was some hope mixed with desperation in her eyes.

The boy looked covetously at Ariella's sword. He was too young to think of real fighting, and she hoped, echoing Peiter's words, that he would never have to. But the child's presence pierced through her veil of loneliness. Perhaps it was worth the risk of another journey.

Ariella gave Jin Lu one of her throwing knives. "I hope you won't need this, but try to practice using it."

The woman took the knife awkwardly. "Thank you," she said. "I will."

Ariella had already made up her mind about this family.

"I will accompany you," she said.

The man bowed. "Thank you, Cashain."

She shook the man's hand, then Jin Lu's. The boy, not wanting to be left out, offered his as well.

CHAPTER 9

The road through the Planes of Korok was wide and level so Ariella was able to ride beside the slow-moving cart and keep up a conversation with Peiter and his family. The chestnut mare she was riding could never compete with the stallion she had had as a baroness, but nevertheless the beast showed some bravery in battle, and Ariella had more or less an understanding with her.

It hadn't rained in days, and the dust was so thick that it was hard to see very far ahead, so she tried to keep alert.

"Cashain, how did you learn to fight?" Seth asked.

Ariella did not reply at first because the roar of a broloug thundered across the plane. The creature couldn't be very near, but the volume of its aggressive growl was formidable. It usually fed on antelopes and pickors and very rarely dined on lone human travelers, so there was little fear of its attacking a group of people, but its powerful roar caused an unconscious terror.

"My nursemaid taught me," she replied at last.

"Your nursemaid!" Seth laughed.

"You wouldn't be laughing if you encountered her in a dark alley."

"Cashain, will you train me when we arrive at my cousin's farm?" the boy asked, "Teach me some swordplay?"

"I won't be able to stay long," she said.

"Why do you have to go?"

"There are other travelers to guard along the road."

"So... you're always traveling back and forth? Isn't it boring? Don't you long for battle?"

She laughed.

The boy's mother tucked him closer to her body, and chided him, "Stop asking silly questions, Seth."

"It's all right," Ariella said, casting another wary look into the distance, "I do long for battle. But that time will come."

She told the boy only the truth. These journeys could not exactly be called dull, she mused as she looked over the desert landscape, what little she could see of it at the moment. Nothing but sand and small stones underfoot. Along the sides of the road there were usually impressively vast expanses of flat land dotted with random rock formations. No greenery save a few small scraggly, thorny shrubs. She often wondered how the pickors and other wild creatures survived on such scant feed.

Instinct suddenly brought her hand to her sword hilt. There were riders behind them, horse hooves she could hear before ever seeing them through the thick dust.

They were coming closer, which was not surprising considering the slow gait of Peiter's two horses.

"I hear it too," Peiter said.

Jin Lu squeezed the boy so close he grimaced and squirmed from her grasp. "That hurts!"

There were definitely sounds of horse hooves, but also the trundle of wheels, which possibly meant it was another convoy of peaceful travelers like them.

"It might be nothing," Ariella said, "It makes for a doubtful ambush if we can hear them at this distance."

Soon the leading horses and wagons became visible in the dusty swirl. Ariella breathed a sigh of relief. It was just a group of traveling merchants.

One of the riders in the vanguard waved to her as the train approached. It was Cuthbert, a warrior she knew since they had traveled together before.

"Looks like you're living up to your name, Cashain," he joked, "Could you not find a more humble traveler to protect?"

"None humbler than you, Cuthbert," she replied easily. They had been trading jibes for many weeks, and she was not easily offended by his humor.

"If those horses can keep up, you could probably join our caravan," Cuthbert said. "I'll check with the high and mighty ones."

He rode back to ask the merchant in charge, and was evidently given confirmation.

"You better go in the back," he advised, "I don't want those nags slowing us down."

Ariella didn't have any particularly clever retort in mind, so she gave him a crooked smile as he rode by. She and the small family were covered in even more dust as the larger caravan passed them. There were about thirty mounted warriors scattered throughout the convoy. The rest were merchants, but even they were armed to the teeth. They were driving six large wagons drawn by strong, well-fed horses.

The sweltering afternoon wore on. The boy fell asleep, lulled by the motion of the wagon, and conversation dwindled. Ariella tried to fend the heavy languidness off as best she could, though the heat and the monotony of the journey were not helping.

The thwack of an arrow on wood startled her.

She looked around wildly, but all she could see was dust. The brigands were hiding in it, and they needed no other cover.

The merchants didn't dawdle, but whipped up their horses at once, and the whole caravan sped forward, even Peiter's two nags bounding at a hearty pace. Peiter handed the reins over to Jin Lu while he drew his sword. In that intense way that time passes during moments of battle, Ariella noticed how nicked the blade was, but Peiter looked like he meant business despite the decrepitude of his armament.

More arrows flew from left and right, revealing the

positions of the enemy all around them.

"Their horses are fast," Ariella shouted over the din of the moving carts, "we won't likely outrun them, but at least we'll be moving targets."

Jin Lu clutched her son, trying to shield him with her body.

The first riders appeared, tearing through the curtain of dust. It was the horse that gave it away. Those squat, stout horses of the Koroi tribes, resilient creatures with great endurance. The rider's attire, short, loose trousers, leather armor, and the way he rode leaning forward in the saddle meant this was a Koroi warrior. He didn't have the usual tattoos on his arms, but everything else was a sure sign. He wore a beautiful helmet with a long green crest.

By the time she realized the fight would be harder than just fending off some bandits, she was already in it. She only had a split second to assess the enemy before his sword clashed with hers as she deflected his strike.

He wasted no time and instead of using his sword again tried to unseat her from the horse using a steel rod with a concave paddle on the end to catch her foot and push her leg over the saddle. And an unseated rider would be little more than dead meat to a Koroi. It was a method she had seen before, and she countered it using another Koroi custom.

This wasn't easy for someone who had not trained for it from a young age like the Koroi riders did, but she leapt from the stirrups onto the saddle and stood up on its worn leather surface. She struck from overhead, using the "higher ground" advantage over her foe. His small horse alert to every little signal, the Koroi swerved aside. In a split second, he hopped up onto his saddle as well.

His spirited grin flashed, so did his blade, reflecting the afternoon sun as he attacked again. Ariella fought back in what she felt was an awkward way, since she was somewhat rusty in the horse acrobatics that were like second nature to these warriors. But her horse never faltered, following the wagon that she was meant to protect.

She caught a glimpse of happenings in the wagon. Two

riders closing in from both sides. Peiter doubled over in pain, an arrow in his arm. Jin Lu clutching her son with one hand, a knife in the other.

Ariella jumped back into the saddle, ducking a slash of her opponent's sword and veering her horse away from him. He pursued her, but her attention was focused on the cart.

One of the assailants had already climbed from his saddle into the moving cart, and Peiter was grappling with him despite his wounded arm.

Seeing that her husband, unable to hold a sword, was fighting a losing battle, Jin Lu ferociously stabbed the assailant in the chest. Meanwhile, Seth picked up his father's sword and hacked at the other man climbing over the side of the cart. The Koroi dodged the blade, laughing at the boy's efforts.

Ariella threw herself at the Koroi. She landed heavily on top of him, hoping to knock him out. But the man still had a lot of life left in him. He pitched her back, and she nearly fell over the edge of the wagon but managed to keep hold of her sword.

Her erstwhile opponent with the green crest caught up to the cart and swung his sword. She parried, barely even looking back. Her only impulse was to protect the family.

But meanwhile, the other Koroi pressed his advantage, tipping her over the edge of the cart. Flying down, she still saw from the corner of her eye her opponent suddenly arching his back as Jin Lu stabbed him from behind.

Ariella was glad she had given her that knife. But she had to focus on her own plight. She hung onto the hard wooden side of the cart with one hand while her legs dragged painfully on the stony ground and her other hand clutched her sword.

What was more, the rider swung at her again, and she had no defence.

He aimed for her hand, trying to make her release her tenuous hold on the cart.

A boyish cry sounded from nearby, and Seth swiped furiously at the rider who almost unseated himself in his hurry to dodge the attack.

Ariella meanwhile pulled herself back up, catching a glimpse of the raider in the cart being thrown by the wayside by Peiter and Jin Lu.

She jumped to her feet, ready to fight the harrying rider with the green-crested helmet, this time without distractions.

Up ahead, the Koroi were attacking richer spoils, but this one seemed to insist on raiding the humble vehicle that was under her protection. Well, he would not be doing it for long.

She reached a hand into her cloak and threw the knife. The Koroi was a dead man for sure.

But instead of crumpling up and dying, he did something Ariella couldn't quite believe. He dodged the knife. No one had ever survived one of her throws. And this particular throw had been a stealthy move mostly hidden within the garment's folds. He had either amazing instincts or magic. He shouted something to his followers who were catching up.

Ariella could understand enough of their language to know that he was commanding his men to capture her. Wasting no time, she lunged at him. The precarious side of the cart, little more than a thin plank, bouncing over the uneven road was not the best platform for fighting a mounted rider, but she had no choice since her horse had drifted back.

Swords clashed with much vigor but little results. Ariella could not find a weakness in the Koroi's defences, and he looked like he was enjoying the bout. She tried to lure him into unbalancing himself in the saddle, but he would not fall for such tricks. He was good, no doubt about it.

Ariella was so occupied with the swordplay that she failed to notice that the other riders closing in had no ordinary weapons until it was too late.

A rope whistled through the air, encircling her body. She slashed through it, setting herself free, but only for a brief moment. More ropes and nets flew at her.

Heavy nets, the cords strengthened with something, tar or burnt oil perhaps. One of the riders pulled hard; she lost her footing and tumbled to the ground. It was not an easy landing. She choked on the billowing dust while sharp stones bit into her back and shoulders.

"Cashain!" Seth shouted, and almost leapt off the cart, but his parents pulled him back.

The despondent faces of the family she was meant to protect looked back at her as the cart rushed away and she was dragged along the ground away from them. But she had done her job after all. The Koroi stopped harrying the cart. All the riders, including the one with the plumed helmet, turned back to her as soon as she fell.

She tried to slash through the nets, but it was hard to get good momentum with the sword. Within a few seconds, it was too late, as it seemed like all the Koroi in the world descended on her, gripping her arms and legs tightly and making escape impossible.

***

Mara took a last look at the trees of the Ringing Woods.

The trees no longer looked to her like they had grotesque human faces. She could feel their sentience and understand their language, so there was no need for them to put on a front for her sake as they had done when she first arrived. They had only done that to scare and mock any passing humans and deter them from entering the forest.

When madness first struck her, she realized that the trees had spirits. But as much as she was curious about them, her mind could not focus on one thing. She saw everything at once. Her past came back so vividly. All the feelings she had run away from, the horrible heartbreak when her lover left her. The devastation when her own family disowned her and the villagers banished her when they found out she was pregnant. The last soft breaths of her dying baby daughter, and the blame she put on herself for not being able to provide the milk to feed her since she herself was starving.

At the same time, the entire world of the present moment rushed in on her and drew her into its maelstrom. The colors of the forest were too bright, the emotions of the people and elves around her touched her as if they were her own. There were too many words in her mind. Everything she had ever heard or said, and then new ones she wanted to say. Whenever she tried to talk, they came out in a stream of nonsense.

She was drawn at once to the trees, their serene spirits. It helped her to calm her raging thoughts and emotions. Slowly, over time, she did not know how many days or weeks or months, she found that the more time she spent sitting beneath the trees the more she could focus and not be lost in the swarm of images and words.

Sometimes Larkos spoke to her, and she found his words soothing. Sometimes she even found the right words to say to him, ones that made sense.

There had not really been a particular day when she realized she was no longer mad because occasionally she still saw visions. But now, she did not let them overwhelm her, and she had made peace with the past. The things she saw now were usually of the present.

"Will I always be haunted by these visions?" she had asked Larkos one day.

"The visions are a gift," he replied. "Eventually you will find them useful, not haunting."

Mara began to understand what he meant when she saw a vision of her two former traveling companions. The lovers had been torn asunder. One was a lord imprisoned in his own palace, the other a lonely traveler, imprisoned in her own despair.

Mara knew the feeling very well. She was not sure what to do or how to find them again, so she traveled to the neighbouring villages, trying to glean some news. The mission turned out to be surprisingly easily accomplished.

People saw her differently now. In her elven garments she appeared a majestic lady, and perhaps some mistook her for an elf. But they did not fear her either. She could easily draw them into conversation, and she soon found out that Ariella had lost her lands and had been taken to Sylcadia by none other than the royal prince himself.

Mara hurried back to the Ringing Woods. In the old days, she simply would have been astounded to find herself hobnobbing with royalty, but now her thoughts were more focused on helping Ariella and Demetrius. The visions told Mara that the warrior maiden had indeed been at the royal court but was all alone now.

She looked for her two best friends, Evoe and Lorel. They were brother and sister, both a little strange, even for elves. When she found him, Evoe was lying on his side and staring intently at something, though she could not see anything there. Nothing around but grass and a few trees.

"Mara, it's good you're back," he said, not taking his gaze from whatever it was. "I am about to make an amazing discovery. I've been looking at this stalk of grass for over an hour, and I thought, 'Is the grass changed by my looking at it, or am I?' And you know what, I think it's both."

"That's amazing!"

"You really think so?" he asked.

"No, not really. Besides, how can the grass be changed by you looking at it?"

"A good question," he said raising his finger in the air. "I don't yet know, but I feel it must."

The two siblings had always been curious about the world, and especially about the human world. That was why Mara counted on them to accompany her on this new journey.

Lorel soon joined them, skipping forth from the deep recesses of the forest.

"Mara! Mara! Mara!" she cried with such joy as if they had not seen each other in years.

"'Tis good to see you too, Lorel," Mara said, touched by the attention. She could not recall anyone being that happy to see her back in the human world, in the former life that seemed a lifetime ago.

The elf maiden hugged her, lifted her off the ground and spun her around.

"What tidings do you bring, my dear Mara?"

"The tidings are not too good for my former companions,"

Mara said, "It's just as I feared, they need my help."

She told them what she had learned from the villagers.

"I've decided to go to Argentz," she concluded, "I will find Demetrius first and see if he can lead me to Ariella. Will you come with me?"

"Of course I'll come with you," Evos said, finally taking his eyes off the plant.

"We will go if Larkos agrees, but I don't think he will," Lorel said with a pout.

"What's gotten up his arse?"

"Mara, sometimes you're just like your old self again," Lorel remarked, "Is that any way to talk about our king?"

"I'm still my old self," Mara said with a mischievous smile, "just with a few more tricks up my beautiful green sleeve."

Larkos let his mind wander over many domains, both physical and spiritual, all while lounging comfortably on a curved bough about a hundred feet above the ground. Being the elf king left him with much more spare time than, say, a human king, and he was spending it doing the equivalent of a human reading a book; only the book he was currently reading was not written on paper, but on the air, in the dust drifting from thousands of miles away, in the echoes of past centuries, and in the secret conduits of the spirit world.

Although he was well-hidden from prying eyes, his green clothing blending into the foliage, he could not hide from Mara. Her powers of perception were so strong now, almost equal to his own. Surprising for a human.

"Larkos! Where are you?"

"You know very well I'm up here," he grumbled.

"It's about Ariella."

"I know," he said sharply.

Mara seemed to divine just as well as he did that Ariella was in danger. Worse than that, the warrior's spirit was broken. He held in his hand a leather band, a keepsake she had given him. Larkos had enchanted it with his magic to keep her doings and feelings closer to him. Now, a sickly green mold infected the fabric, and it had been there a few days. It was a sign of something terribly wrong.

"Why don't you come down?" Mara called.

Evidently her madness had been cured, but not her cheekiness.

"Is this how you talk to the elf king?" he replied. "Come up here if you wish to speak to me."

"Don't think I won't!"

He could hear her cursing below, but her small, slender body was well up to the task of climbing the tree with almost elf-like skill.

"I'd like to help her," Mara continued, slightly breathless from the climb, taking a seat on a branch a little below his. "She saved me by bringing me here, gave me a new life. I must repay the favor."

"Well, why have you come to me then?" he said impatiently. He would not admit to anyone how much he cared about Ariella, perhaps not even to himself. He had only known her a few days. She was a human. But somehow, the memory would not fade, much as he tried to distract himself with matters both near and far.

"Maybe you can help too?" Mara asked, this time her tone a little more respectful.

"There is nothing I can do," Larkos replied. "She's hiding. She doesn't want help. She wants to get away from everything and everyone that caused her pain."

"Do you know where she is?"

"Even if I did know, I wouldn't tell you," he said. "Look, even if I went there myself, it wouldn't help her."

"Maybe if some of her friends were there..."

"You mean him."

Larkos turned towards the tree trunk, pretending to study its bark. Although he had the gift of knowing the past and divining events happening at a distance, he could not see into the future except for rare flashes. It was murky at best. Even so, he knew his hopes for seeing Ariella again and winning her favor had little basis in reality. As much as he desired her, as much as she was intrigued by him, he could sense when they first met, and even now, how overwhelmingly strong her love was for that human, and it had only grown stronger over time.

"We could try to reunite them," Mara suggested carefully.

"Then it's up to you. I will not lift a finger to do it."

"Because you are so terribly busy here?" she asked.

"Getting cheeky again, are we? In fact, I am busy. I sense a visitor arriving, several visitors. They have already crossed into my domain."

"Sure, a bunch of squirrels. How exciting for you!"

"Mara, get off my tree."

He knew that despite all her impudence Mara wouldn't dare to mention the real reason why he refused to help, even if she did know it.

"Oh all right," she said, beginning the climb down, "I see you're no use anyway."

"Wait!" he commanded. "I meant what I said about you helping her. I know Ariella would be happy to see you again. You should make that journey."

Mara paused, her usually roguish expression turning more serious.

"What if I did want to... reunite them?"

Larkos tried to stifle a tortured sigh, but he could not contain it. His heart burned with jealousy.

"Do what you think is right," he said. "You can even take an escort of elves with you, if they wish to go on this journey. The only thing I cannot do is come with you. My duty is to stay with my elves and watch over them."

Mara nodded.

"I'll leave at once."

"I wish I could come with you," Larkos whispered when she was out of hearing.

But the visitors whose arrival he had sensed were very real, not just an excuse, and he knew their plight was urgent. He was about to climb down from the tree when he spotted a mounted company of his elves approaching.

Their graceful steeds danced impatiently beneath the tree, but Larkos did not make them wait long. He moved quickly from branch to branch, and in a few seconds, he was on the ground.

"Shall we greet the humans?" Theodre asked. He was a healer, and his skills would probably be needed. Many of the elves sensed that the group of humans arriving was in need of assistance.

"Yes, this should be most interesting," Larkos said, mounting the horse they had brought for him.

The ride didn't take long. The trees were perturbed by the newcomers. They communicated their displeasure to each other through signals that were clear to elf ears. The cavalcade rode in elven fashion, fading from the solid physical realm and passing like air through shrubs, trees, and all obstacles.

They startled the humans, who must have thought they appeared out of nowhere when they materialized before them.

A sorry bunch they looked, weary and in pain. A dozen or so men, six women and one boy made up the numbers of the company, and most of them did not look like they could put up much of a fight. Their clothes bore scorch marks, and their faces showed apprehension and despair as they halted their slow plod through the forest.

When they saw the elves, a few tried to run, but their leader stopped them.

"It's no use," he said. "We are in the Ringing Woods now, and there's no hiding from the elves."

He stepped forward to greet the elves, and made a solemn bow.

"My name is Vidor, and I humbly ask your hospitality in these woods."

Larkos grinned wickedly. "Vidor, we meet at last. I've heard of you and your inn."

"It was burned to the ground, alas."

"I'm sorry to hear it. But glad you finally found the courage to enter my domain. I know you may have heard some unflattering things about elves. You live almost on the edge of my forest, but have never paid a visit. I would almost think it... discourteous."

"You seem to know a lot about me, your majesty. Then you must also know I'm a rebel, fleeing the king's wrath. I knew one day I may have to seek shelter in your woods, and yes, I did fear what I might find here. But I would never give King Theodos the satisfaction of catching me. So now that I'm here, do your worst, but whatever you do, please do not send me back to Chaldea."

This little speech made Larkos and the elves laugh uncontrollably.

"Do our worst?" Larkos said. "Did you hear that, Theodre?"

"He thinks very poorly of us indeed."

"Follow me, then," the king commanded.

The elves walked their horses towards the cabins they had set up for guests. The humans trudged listlessly behind them.

"The gods of the forest may forgive us if we dispense with the hunt," Larkos whispered to his companions, "These poor souls have been through enough already, and I have a feeling they are needed elsewhere in the human world. I think the only thing to do is feed them."

"But first, I should take care of those burns," Theodre said.

"And then we shall feast," Larkos declared.

Although slightly wary at first, the humans began to devour the meal set up for them in the clearing a few hours later. Theodre had treated and bandaged their burns. The people whose clothes were damaged in the fire now wore beautiful elven garments.

Vidor sat in the place of honor beside the king, but in spite of everything Larkos could read his mind, filled with distrust of the elves.

"What is it that caused such enmity between you and the royal house?" Larkos asked, knowing it's a subject he would warm up to.

"It was not enmity, precisely," the innkeeper explained, "not at first. It was simply that I wanted to support the little man, you know? Those who have nothing, or those who have lost their livelihood. Sometimes they turned to crime, and the king's laws had no sympathy for such folk. The king himself was not bad as far as kings go, King Acheron, that is. Meaning no offence to you!"

"None taken," Larkos grinned, "I think you'll find an elf king is much different from a human one. We have better fashion, for one."

"I'll say," Vidor agreed, casting an admiring gaze on the king's silver robe, "I have an eye for fashion, it's all part of producing great theater. And aside from that, you have been nothing if not kind."

"But go on, you were talking about King Acheron."

"Well, as I say, King Acheron, I had little quarrel with. And he had little quarrel with me. His son, that's another matter."

"I didn't like the look of him either," Larkos said.

This hardly ever happened to him, but suddenly a vision of the future flashed unbidden into his mind. The vision had come and gone so suddenly that even Vidor noticed Larkos' amazement.

"What is it, your majesty?" he asked.

Larkos put down his goblet. This would not be easy to put into words, but he knew now exactly what to do with the innkeeper.

"You are a rebel..." he began.

"In my own way. I know it may seem strange to some, but I try to do what I'm good at. And what I'm good at happens to be staging erotic plays."

"Your inn was a remarkable place. Like everything, it had to come to an end. But I think your days as a rebel are not over. I think you may be of some help to Ariella."

"Who is Ariella?"

"You've met her before. She passed through your inn one night, and she is the reason the king's retribution has fallen on you."

"Ah, the beatiful lady. I don't hold it against her. In fact, I'm flattered that sheltering her made Theodos angry enough to come in person and burn down my inn."

"She is a rebel too, and I have a feeling you must both help each other."

"Your majesty, I am flattered, but I'm a mere innkeeper. I have always done my part by sheltering those who needed shelter. But do you expect me to play an active role in fighting monarchs and destroying empires?"

"I would never ask anyone to become something they're not. You may rest here a few days. But soon you may want to set up your usual business someplace else, somewhere far from Chaldea."

"It may not be easy. I failed to save my jewellery chest from the fire. Perhaps I'm not such a great businessman after all."

"That can be remedied," Larkos said.

He could not hide from his feelings anymore. It was true that he should not leave his elven domain to interfere in human affairs. But he knew now he had to help her, even if it was done indirectly through others, even if it broke his heart.

CHAPTER 10

The caravan was safe, but the sense of relief Ariella experienced was soon replaced by worries about her own fate. The merchandise had been saved, so had the small family she fought for. This time, the Koroi seemed satisfied with capturing a few other convoy guards along with Ariella, to sell as slaves most likely.

Bound hand and foot, she was thrown over a horse as if she was a pickor carcass and thus transported to the Koroi encampment. It was a fairly short but uncomfortable ride that took them to a huge congregation of tents by a stream nestled between two hills.

Here, the prisoners were each taken to a separate tent. Ariella lost sight of the man in green-crested helmet, and warriors took her to where she was meant to wait, a storage tent holding sacks of something that felt like flour as far as she could tell when she was thrown down onto them.

It was a long time before an old woman came with a cup of water which barely relieved her thirst. Then she was left alone again, and the hours crawled by. She felt little trepidation, for the blank shroud of non-feeling proved a good ally in this predicament.

As the light outside the tent began to wane, there were finally footsteps coming closer. She wondered if it was the man she had fought. She was curious about him.

But the figure of the man who entered was completely different. A tall and ungainly form pushed through the tent flap, and she saw the man from the Sprightly Pig, the one with all the strange warnings, looming above her.

"I told you chivalry could get you killed," he said.

This could not be good. She did not know whether he had talked to her that day purely by chance and he was already planning to rob the caravan or whether his decision to make the raid was driven by capturing her in particular. She didn't like the way he was looking at her now. Too much like a lustful beast.

"Well, I'm not dead yet," she said flatly.

"You will be if you keep up this contrary spirit. You're mine now, princess. And you thought the borderlands couldn't touch you."

"I can see what kind of 'merchant' you are, a slaver."

She wanted to spit in disgust, but her mouth was too dry.

"People are a commodity as good as any, better, in fact. They bring a hefty amount of gold. But I don't have to sell you if I find that your behavior improves. My name is Howell, I could be your new master. I know I must teach you a lesson first because you're obviously a stubborn one. Soon you'll learn to obey..."

That look was in his eye still, even more intense now. He came closer.

Ariella was not up for much fighting. Her ribs felt bruised from the ride, and her back and shoulders ached from falling and being dragged along the ground.

But this was beyond all boundaries.

Despite her feet being tied together, she could still kick. She aimed at his knee as he approached, and nearly hit the mark. He moved aside, fairly agile for all his large girth.

Then he straddled her, foiling any further attempts at kicking. With one of his huge hands he held her wrists, while the other sought to tear her tunic and hose. She writhed like mad, but his sheer weight was crushing. She had no breath to fight. With one last effort, she twisted her wrists out of his grasp and elbowed him in the nose.

Blood flowed from his nostrils, and he rolled to the side, nursing his injury.

"That's good, keep fighting," he muttered, "You're only whetting my appetite."

He recovered quickly and came back at her with a hard back-handed slap to her face.

"You know how this ends, don't you?" he taunted.

Ariella saved her breath for the fight. Confronted with the dark realization that he would not give up, she knew she had to kill him. But there was no weapon at hand, even her attacker had none that she could appropriate. The only way to do it would be to strangle him in a headlock or to break his neck.

The circumstances were not exactly in her favor, but if she didn't let Howell crush her with his weight again, she stood a chance.

Now, he was enraged. He tried for another slap, but Ariella evaded it and blocked all the blows that came at her. He attempted to crush her again as she knew he would, but she rolled off the stack of flour sacks, taking him with her.

As they landed in a tangled heap, Ariella found the next best thing to strangling him, which was to pin his neck against the ground with her forearm. But Howell was too strong. His face turning red, he still managed to throw her aside, and then he was on top of her again.

Two punches to the face made her too dazed to resist as his hands reached under her clothes and clawed loathsomely against her bare skin.

"What in the name of Bai Meng is going on there?" a man's voice shouted from somewhere nearby. "I thought we were feasting."

The man who stumbled through the opening of the tent wore the short green and beige tunic of a high-ranking Koroi chieftain, though none of the requisite tattoos on his arms. Ariella thought she recognized his face too, at least the bottom half of his face. It was the one she had fought, the one with the green-crested helmet. He swayed drunkenly, but didn't seem completely out of his senses. His keen, black eyes set above high cheek bones looked calm.

"Stop your unseemly marring of the goods," he commanded.

Howell barely gave him a look.

"Why should I?"

"For one thing, as the saying goes, only a fool tries to make a pet out of a broloug. The desert will laugh at you. And for another, half the merchandise is mine."

Howell ignored him and kept up the struggle, groping her body with his hateful hands.

"I said let her go. Do not make me draw this blade," the Koroi warned, his hand at his sword hilt, "once freed from its confines, it will have to taste blood before it returns to the scabbard."

Howell glared at him with the rage of a wild animal deprived of it meat, but evidently decided not to provoke his host. His grip slackened, and Ariella fell back, her head throbbing.

"I will speak with Cashain alone," the man said.

As the sound of Howell's footsteps crunching on the stones outside died away, the Koroi man sat down beside her.

"He's a dull old fellow," the chieftain remarked as Ariella lay there, panting from the struggle, "He hates women, which makes me dislike him. But unfortunately he is one of the few merchants around these parts who will deal with me, a 'barbarian'. Beggars can't be choosers. I'm the youngest son of the Great Toroi, the Chief or our tribes. My name is Riobard."

"I don't suppose you'd like to untie me, Riobard," she suggested.

"Maybe," he said, "depends on how our conversation goes."

"Well?" Having caught her breath, Ariella shifted to a less awkward position leaning back against the sacks. She was shaking all over, and she hoped the Koroi would not notice it, being tipsy as he was.

"You're not going to thank me for saving you there?"

Ariella glared at him. "You're the one who captured me and put me in this position, so no. Besides, I could have killed him myself."

"I think I've heard of you," the chieftain said musingly, "and not just as Cashain, protector of humble travelers. You fought against us a few years ago, riding with the queen of Dezearre. Young and inexperienced, yet very dangerous. Some of my men recognized you."

"Why do you care who I am?"

"Because I need allies. I mean to conquer your Northern Coast, and someone like you, a warrior woman of Dezearre, could help me."

"That's very bold."

"I'm a bold fellow," he replied readily. "And I see you have a magical talisman. I wouldn't know how to use it or even dare touch it myself..." he produced the leather pouch which held her crystal. "But it would be extremely useful too in my conquest if you were to wield it under my banners."

"I ride under no one's banners," Ariella replied, "those days are over."

"Even if it meant taking revenge on those who wronged you? I'm assuming that is the case because otherwise you wouldn't be here, helping travelers out of the kindness of your heart."

Ariella grinned. Although his offer was tempting, and seemed to be an earnest one, she could not ride back into Dezearre like a traitor who had joined the Koroi hordes. There had to be another way.

"Those travelers were escaping the likes of you, a glorified brigand, and you'd like me to ride right back into Dezearre and pillage those same people I had helped to protect?"

"Yes, that's the idea." He tried again, in a more serious tone. "Look, my older brothers have all the land, and they fight amongst themselves for it. That's why the people are fleeing; that's not my fault. But I'm a high-born chieftain, and I need to carve out some land of my own."

"I like you, Riobard," she said, "You don't seem like a complete scoundrel, so I will tell you the truth. I was once a baroness with my own domain, and I served the queen of Dezearre. But she has betrayed me, and now I serve no one but myself. I will take my revenge on her, but in my own time, in my own way."

"The right time may never come."

"I think it will," she insisted, "and now is not the time."

Riobard shook his head in dismay. "Too proud for your own good. Well, there is a remedy for that. And although I cannot use you as an ally, I can sell you for a hefty price. At least I'll get some money to finance my conquest. And I know just the man to sell you to."

"Do with me what you will," Ariella said.

The familiar pall of indifference enveloped her once again.

The slave owner who purchased her was a dour man. A half-dwarf, she guessed, judging by his exceptionally short stature and his long beard. Such beards were not in fashion among humans, and only someone with dwarf blood would wear one that long.

They untied her feet so she could ride, though her hands were fastened together. But she had little hope of escaping on the journey because the slaver was accompanied by an armed escort of twenty tough-looking characters.

"Where are we going?" Ariella asked.

"Back to Nor Kemur, where do you think?" the half-dwarf replied gruffly. "It's the only place anyone can more or less survive in around here."

"I'm guessing you don't particularly like it there?" she asked conversationally.

"No one likes it there. Do you think anyone comes here by choice?"

"Let me guess, you were not wanted in the dwarf community so you made your own way in the world?"

He spat on the ground, maybe trying to stifle some old

memory.

"You've figured it out, look who's so quick. If you were half as quick as you think you are, you wouldn't have been caught for a slave, would you?"

"Fair point," Ariella admitted.

"Now listen, my name is Tazain. I organize fights. Folk around here want to see good-looking women fighting. I provide that spectacle for them. I paid a ridiculous price for you, and I better make my money back, and more. You're supposed to be some kind of great fighter. So fight good, don't let your face get ruined, and you'll make me lots of money."

"Sounds wonderful," she stated, "but what do I get in return?"

"You won't get beaten or starved or killed. Now save your breath for the cage."

"Any chance of release for good behaviour?"

"Stop pestering me, woman. No one gets released. Not unless you make me so much money that I could buy Chaldea."

"I'll see what I can do."

"If you don't stop talking, my guards will beat you."

So this is what it's like to be a slave, Ariella mused. Interesting. She couldn't quite feel anything even despite this dire circumstance, but she was curious. And a feeling of curiosity was a good sign.

She had no desire to be rebellious, at least not yet, so she kept quiet for the rest of the journey. Although she could have attempted an escape into the open plains, it would have been a risky venture. She waited to see what would transpire in Nom Kemur.

The abode where Tazain kept his slaves was an underground chamber, pleasantly cool in the midday heat, but dark and filled with echoes and foul smells. The echoes were mostly of women's voices and her own footsteps as she and her guards strode down a row of cages. She couldn't see the other women clearly in the low light, but could hear fragments of their talk, some casual, some quarrelsome and challenging.

None of them addressed her.

She was pushed into a small cage, just slightly shorter than her height, with a blanket on the earth floor for bedding and a fairly shallow latrine hole. So that was where the smells came from.

"Getting to know different cells of the world," she murmured, recalling her brief stay in prison courtesy of Demetrius' mother.

"Ain't that my life's story?" a woman's voice called out from nearby.

"Have you done anything to deserve it?" Ariella asked. Her eyes had not yet adjusted to the low light, and she only saw an outline of a stocky woman sitting cross-legged on the floor in the cage next to hers.

"'Course. Thieving and plundering and fighting. What about you?"

"Much the same kind of thing," Ariella replied.

"Don't seem like it. You sound like a well-to-do lady."

"We gentlefolk do all the same things, just on a bigger scale."

The woman laughed uproariously. "How do you like this bird of fancy plumage?"

"Shut up, Gerta!" said a deep female voice from father off, "I'm miserable enough in this hell hole without your cackling."

"Don't mind Penelope," the one called Gerta advised, "she's always bad tempered. And I say, why fret since your life is over anyway?"

"That's a cheerful way to look at it," Ariella muttered.

Her eyes adjusting to the low light, she discerened Penelope's bulky form reclining on the floor three cages away. Gerta's dark hair was matted and filthy, her clothes nothing but rags that barely covered her ample breasts and broad thighs. She had a prominent, curved nose, full lips, and a face not harmonious looking but strangely appealing.

"We'll see how you hold up after a few days in here," Penelope remarked in her gruff voice.

Gerta crawled to the bars between them to take a closer

look at the newcomer.

"Oh gods, your face!"

Ariella realized her entire face must look bruised thanks to Howell.

"Did you get... raped?" Gerta whispered.

"No," Ariella said, shuddering inwardly. She felt lucky to have escaped, but she still wished she could wash the foul touch of his hands from her body and the memory from her mind, "Will I be sent to fight soon, up there?"

There was another cage on the main floor above, she knew from talk she had heard in town, though she had never been interested enough to see it for herself, where women would fight, crowds would be entertained, and bets would be made on the winners.

"Soon enough," Gerta replied.

***

Demetrius found his father sitting by his bedside when he awoke. On the other side of the bed, a physician. Both looked pale and weary in the morning sun.

His father smiled warmly on seeing him awaken. The physician looked gratified, as if the credit was all due to him, but Demetrius knew who had helped pull him back from the brink of death. He had seen her in the dream, and after that he felt his spirit had been reprieved. He wanted to live, and the rest was simply combatting the physical infection.

"You've slept three nights straight," his father said. "It's so good to see you awake."

"It felt like one night," Demetrius said hoarsely.

"Well, I shall leave you, Your Majesty" the physician stood up from his chair, "His Highness is certainly out of danger now. The fever is very mild and will soon abate."

"Thank you for your care," the king said. "It will not be forgotten."

"Well," he turned to Demetrius, "I knew you did not survive years of slavery only to die on us now."

"Maybe the years of slavery had something to do with this," Demetrius said.

"I know," said his father, to his surprise. "So many years of exile must always leave a trace. And I am sorry we were unable to free you. As you know, we tried through diplomatic means, but King Acheron would not let you go, and we could not go to war again."

"Father, I never held you responsible. You did the right thing for the kingdom." Besides, his unspoken sentiment was that it was the queen's decision anyway.

"Your mother will be here soon," Gaufridus said, as if reading his mind. "She has not had much rest since your illness began, and this is the first night I persuaded her to get some sleep."

"Before she arrives, I would like to ask you one thing."

The king preempted his question.

"I don't know where Ariella is. After the trial, she left the palace. Left the city, I expect."

"And you don't know where she went?"

"No, honestly, I do not. I can see this troubles you, and I would tell you if I knew anything."

Demetrius believed his father. But his mother might have more information, not that she would reveal it of course. The fact that she would put Ariella on trial told him just how far his mother was willing to go to eliminate Edoline's rival. It would probably be useless to talk to her, but despite everything, he had to try.

Of course, he did not broach the subject at once.

The first day was too exhausting and he was barely able to walk to the window of his chamber, much less confront his mother. But in the following week, he slowly recovered his strength, and the fever was at last completely gone.

The queen came to see him, sitting by his bedside and sharing the afternoon meal in his chamber. It was mostly soup, as the physicians did not advise any rich food.

"You look well today," she said.

"I feel well," he confirmed. "Thank you for not looking

116

down upon this humble repast, mother."

"Of course. Forgoing heavy food is the least I can do for you."

He did not want to upset the peaceful balance of this moment. Her lovely face, slightly pinched with age, now looked even more pinched, all on account of worrying about him. But he had to ask her.

"Mother, is there truly no news of Ariella? Did she leave without any of her people?"

"And I thought you might have asked about Edoline."

"What could possibly happen to Edoline? I know you haven't let her see me yet because of all that's happened."

"You're most astute," the queen replied, putting down her plate. "Perhaps Edoline took things too far, the trial and all that..."

"And you allowed it."

"I'm sorry, I thought it was best. But now, I expected you to be satisfied knowing that Ariella is safe, away from all the trouble at court, trouble she brought upon herself, I might add."

"But I don't know she's safe. I don't even know where she is."

"And if I tell you, no doubt you will wish to go see her again."

Demetrius was silent, trying to decide on his best option. Revealing his desire would be a mistake, but it seemed his mother already knew it. Either way, he lost.

"I might be satisfied with sending a glider," he suggested.

"We both know that's not true."

"So you won't tell me, but you admit you know where she is."

"I admit nothing."

"How very like you, mother. I know, maybe you'll tell me if I agree to marry Edoline. Is that your little plan?"

"No, it isn't, but now that you mention it, would you make that trade?"

Demetrius lay back on his pillows. The illness had taken a

toll on his strength, and recovery was slow and exhausting. Even his thoughts were slow and heavy.

"I wonder..." he asked, "during my absence did you come to see Edoline as a sort of replacement for me? Is that why you won't let her go and must have me marry her? Do you love her more than your own child?"

The queen seemed outraged and didn't speak for a few moments, gasping for words. Demetrius could not tell whether it was in earnest.

"How can you say that to me?" she pronounced at last.

"It's all right. I don't begrudge you your daughter. Let her inherit the throne in my stead, I care not."

"You would care if you weren't rendered mad by your illness."

"Now I'm mad, am I?"

"It's the only explanation I can find to your refusal to do your royal duty."

She rose from the chair and was about to leave the chamber, but she turned around.

"I hate to do this, but I have been prepared for this eventuality..."

"What do you mean?" Demetrius asked.

"I see that this woman still has a hold over you, and I cannot allow you to endanger the kingdom. Therefore, you will not leave this chamber until I have your word of honor that you'll agree to marry Edoline."

"What nonsense is this, by all the living stars?"

Demetrius rose from the bed and opened the door, only to find two guards outside it. From their presence and their guilty looks he could tell the situation was serious.

"I'm sorry, Your Highness," one of the men said.

"It's not your fault," Demetrius replied, glaring at his mother.

She walked past him to exit the chamber.

"I know you think me cold and indifferent, but I do care," she said in the doorway, "and this is what's best for the realm, for you, for everyone. By the way, Ariella has gone to Castle

Reimfred, just as we planned. She wanted to be alone, and I thought it was an excellent idea."

CHAPTER 11

The days went by in the fetid stench of the cell, and in the sweaty, vomit-inducing, clamouring hall with the iron cage where Ariella fought.

She fought bare-handed with her fists, she wrestled, and on very rare occasions she fought with a weapon in hand. Mostly, the fights were meant to provoke feelings of sensuality rather than violence from the rough and ready crowd. Fighters were expensive to procure, and usually Tazain and the few other slave owners tried to avoid a death match. But at the same time, the fights had to be real. Anyone seen to be not trying hard enough would be thoroughly beaten by Tazain's guards after the official fight was over.

Despite it all, Ariella felt hopeful. Slowly, ever so slowly, some remnants of feelings were awakening inside her. She could even find solace in talking with the other slaves and some sympathy for them. She especially liked Gerta and her grim sense of humor as well as her more serious moments.

"It's only the thought of breaking out of here one day that keeps me going," Gerta confessed to her one day, "Not that I ever will, but that's how my mind keeps me alive, I guess."

"Do you have a home to go back to?" Ariella asked.

"No, not really, but freedom would be enough."

"You're lucky," Ariella said.

"Why, what do you mean?"

Ariella thought of Queen Esclairmonde many miles away in her royal palace.

"I need more than freedom. I need revenge."

"Revenge, that's something," Gerta remarked, trying to get comfortable as she leaned back against the bars of her cell. "You think beyond a day or two into the future, which is more than I can say for the usual ruffians one encounters around here."

Usually she fought slaves that had been freshly brought in to Tazain's establishment, or even ones owned by other masters willing to risk the fighting cages. She rarely had to face off against someone she knew well. But when there was a lull in new slaves, Ariella was ordered to fight Gerta.

That night she could hardly sleep, despite her opponent trying to assuage her doubts.

"Fight me as hard as you can," Gerta insisted, "Don't worry about anything else. If Tazain sees you're not trying, we'll both get a beating afterward."

It was something Ariella would recall later only as a nightmarish vision. The crowd's roar, egging her on to hurt her friend in the enclosed space of the iron cage. The smell of sweat from hundreds of unwashed bodies. The drumming of her heart.

She was tempted not to try at all, to take any punishment Tazain would dole out afterward, but she feared Gerta would then be punished as well.

The brawl began, and Ariella dealt some punches and took some punches. She was trying not to think beyond protecting her face, but her instincts guided her to gain the advantage. In the end, Ariella was declared the winner. As usual, the clinking of coins mixed with cries of triumph and despair as bets were won and lost.

Gerta kneeled on the arena, too exhausted to stand. Her lip was bleeding, and she was doubled over in pain.

"Remind me never to fight you again," she panted, "And

don't look so sour, it's not your fault. They forced us to do it."

"Soon, they will pay," Ariella whispered.

Escape plans, however, were not going very well.

She tried digging at the earth floor, only to discover it was underlaid by stone, tried seducing the guards, but they knew better than to fall for the women in their charge. The options were dwindling, but she did not give up hope. There had to be a way she had not thought of yet.

But in the next few days, she was distracted by an alarming piece of news. Tazain himself came down to their cells in person to tell her. He rarely made visits to the cells, and she had not seen much of him. Observing his leisurely stroll along the rows of cages, his immaculate attire of leather and silk, his obvious indifference to the slaves and their paltry condition, she hated him.

This was actually good. She was beginning to feel again. She wished hatred would not be the feeling to bring her back to life, but here it was, and it was not unwelcome.

"Cashain," he said, stopping in front of her cage. "You will fight the new champion whose name is Magdelne. She is formidable, I can tell you. She fights with a giant hammer, and when she's finished nothing is left alive, to put it mildly. It's going to be a death match. But I know you will triumph, Cashain, my loyal hound. Well, aren't you going to say anything?"

Ariella was seething. Now she had to kill another woman of Dezearre, especially one with the same name as one who had taken her in and cared for her.

"I don't want to kill for entertainment," she replied, not looking at him, "Must it be to the death?"

"You disappoint me, Cashain. I was expecting something along the lines of 'I'll do my best for you, master. I'll destroy her.'"

"If it's to the death, I'll need to prepare," Ariella said, glancing at him to judge his reaction, "Can I see her fight?"

"Hm, hm, at least you're taking this fight seriously. I'll see what I can do."

Without any words of farewell, he left her to her thoughts. Maybe observing the other fighter would give her an opportunity to escape. To be taken outside of her usual cell could be her chance.

It was a few days later that she was taken to Tazain's private balcony to observe the fight away from the rabble below. When she was led out to see her opponent, there were two guards flanking her and many more guards all around, but in any case Ariella became too distracted by the horrible sight before her to contemplate escape.

"Mag-delne! Mag-delne! Mag-delne!" the crowd cheered as the giant woman with the hammer, seemingly oblivious to the noise, dealt her deadly blows.

The two other women in the cage with her tried to work as a team, one distracting her while the other struck, but she was fast enough to counter them both. The audience was usually content to sit at their tables and drink, but this evening they clung to the walls of the cage with fascinated interest.

Aside from being made of muscle, standing over six feet tall, and wielding a huge steel hammer, Magdelne was a good fighter. She made no mistakes. Ariella had been hoping to see a weak point by watching her fight, but found none.

Magdelne's opponents did make mistakes, and it cost them dearly. One got off easy with a broken forearm, the other met the force of the hammer with her skull, only a bloody mass remaining of her head. The woman who remained alive crouched in the corner, whimpering. Magdelne was about to finish her off, but guards intervened and led her away. The fight was over.

Ariella was in a fairly brooding mood when she returned to her cell.

"How was she?" Gerta asked.

Ariella shook her head. "I wish I hadn't seen it."

Two days later, the fight was set to begin. Ariella was waiting to be led out of her cage after the evening meal. She had tried to remain hopeful. Everyone had a weakness, and surely so did Magdelne; she just hadn't seen it yet. She would have to try to reveal it, while not getting herself crushed by that deadly hammer.

Gerta seemed as nervous as she was. The usually hearty woman ate slowly and pensively, not saying much.

"Do you have a strategy?" Gerta finally asked.

"Gods, you're looking at me like it's my funeral. I'll have to keep her at a distance, that's all I know. I've gone over it in my mind, but there's nothing I can see until I actually face her."

Gerta came over to the cell wall and reached her hand through the bars to touch her shoulder.

"Well... don't die. The rest of these vixens are no fun at all."

"I heard that!" Penelope called.

At last she was taken to the dark closet-like space where the fighters waited to come into the cage.

The massive outline of her opponent loomed from the shadows; even sitting down on a bench, she looked tall. She had a forbidding face with a strong brow and a stern gaze.

Ariella succumbed to her nervous habit of making terrible jokes, taking the bench across from her.

"Gods, woman, did your parents not feed you enough?"

But her opponent sat rigidly silent. This did nothing to relive the tension, and Ariella couldn't stop herself from talking.

"Are you going to fight by the rules of honor or should I expect kicking and biting?"

At last, the woman looked at her, a heavy gaze filled with condemnation.

"You so-called noble ladies, you speak of honor, but you have none."

"You may be right," Ariella shrugged.

"Are you trying to sweeten me up so I won't kill you? It won't work. The fight is to the death. Why do you even care about your life? It can't be all that magnificent if you've ended up in this hole."

"I must live to take revenge against my enemies."

"Enemies..." the woman laughed bitterly. "Might as well take revenge against the whole world. Not one human being is your friend, not really."

"That is a bitter lesson to learn. Part of me thought so too, but I want to think there are still good people in the world. And although we don't all act as honorably as we should, maybe to strive for honor is the important thing."

The giantess shrugged her massive shoulders.

"Why strive for honor when it's all meaningless?"

Ariella hoped it wasn't so. "I don't know if it's all meaningless or not," she said. All she could think was why would the gods grant someone so bitter such strength and put a hammer in her hand?

"You think you'll be the one to survive, don't you?" the woman said after a pause. "Well," she shrugged again, "every fighter's heart longs to win, but fate decides."

The patrons were more rowdy than usual this night. They could smell blood. This being a fight to the death, the stakes were higher. The betting didn't stop even as the women entered the cage.

Magdelne had her hammer, and Ariella had been given a serviceable enough sword, not a two handed one like she preferred, but it would have to do.

"Begin!" Tazain commanded from his balcony.

Magdelne roared into action, and it was all Ariella could do to stay out of her way. She did not even try to parry the heavy blows of the hammer for fear of being unbalanced. Dodging this way and that, she stayed out of reach.

By doing this she was enraging her opponent.

"Enough dancing!" Magdelne shouted.

Maybe this could be the key, Ariella thought, letting her tire herself out and make a mistake out of sheer rage or exhaustion.

"It's not my fault if you're too slow to follow the dance," Ariella teased.

The swinging hammer came dangerously close.

Ariella still retreated, but she suddenly realized Magdelne did not let anger force her into making a blunder. The woman knew exactly what she was doing, herding Ariella into the corner of the cage.

This left her no choice. She swung out with the sword to gain some distance, and Magdelne swatted it aside. The audience roared as steel rang against steel. The battle was engaged.

Hammer collided with sword, but just as she had feared, each swing of the hammer drove Ariella off balance, leaving her vulnerable and making her tend again to retreat. She tried to circle Magdelne instead of being backed into a corner. She hoped her opponent would tire, but it was not to be, or at least not so soon. The hammer struck with relentless rhythm.

Before she knew it, her back was against the wall of the cage. Their weapons locked together, Ariella tried to push back, but the accursed woman was so strong she would not budge an inch. One small step to the side would have taken her to safety, but before she could move, Magdelne pushed forward all her formidable strength onto the haft of the hammer and drove Ariella's own sword into her face. Magdelne was about to follow up with a crushing blow, but as she wound up for the kill, Ariella rolled away to escape.

The steel of the hammer rang against the iron of the cage, deafening the fighters even more than the excited roar of the audience.

Ariella got back on her feet, cursing. Pain wove a long, burning thread down the right side her face. Blood ran from her forehead and into her eye. She swiped at it to clear her vision. Aside from the thought that this would completely disfigure her, which she pushed aside for the moment, the loss of blood could be serious enough to weaken her. She had to end this quickly, or she was dead.

Ariella lashed out in utter fury, and Magdelne went on the defensive. For the moment, Ariella gained some ground and had the center of the arena to herself. She had been afraid for far too long. Afraid of her own feelings. Now, for a brief moment her feelings flared up like a fire suddenly given fuel. Her fury shouted at her to rule this tiny and pathetic kingdom of the cage. There were other kingdoms to get to, but this came first.

Ariella knew how dangerous fury could be in a fight. But it could also be helpful if reined in and used only to enhance the strength of her attacks.

Then the idea came to her. Of course, the only way to win was to topple the giantess. It was risky, but then she had nothing to lose except plenty of blood.

After a rest of mere seconds that seemed much too short, Ariella made the first attack. She finally saw a glimmer of hope that Magdelne was not made of steel; she was obviously growing short on breath.

Ariella made as if trying to push her back with an aggressive lunge. Magdelne gave way just a little, and in the moment when she lifted her foot off the ground, Ariella stepped around her and kicked her knee out from under her while pulling down on her upper body. Magdelne toppled with a satisfying thud, but she was not defenceless.

There was no way to win without making a sacrifice.

Ariella realized it in that very moment as she could see from the corner of her eye that Magdelne swung from her low position that there was not time for defence. She had to end it here and now while her opponent was at a disadvantage, and she did nothing to move out of the way. Instead, she focused on making the kill as she stabbed straight down at Magdelne's chest. Her sword pierced the leather armor and found the heart.

Magdelne's shocked expression testified to the fatal wound.

At the same time, the sickening crunch of bone filled the hall. Ariella collapsed, in complete agony, her shin shattered by the hammer. Her cry of pain drowned out by shouts from the excited audience, she fell beside her stricken foe. Everything became a blur outside of the horrible throbbing in her leg, but she managed to say to Magdelne just before the defeated woman's stern eyes grew dim, "You will be avenged."

***

Demetrius was growing restless.

His confinement made it impossible to get a message out. His loyal servant had been replaced with a new imperturbable and unbribable one. The guards were equally honest in carrying out their duty and unwilling to help him. Fighting the guards could be suicidal, for he did not have his sword and armor.

The only way he had to communicate with Ariella would be the glider, which could enter through his window, but for whatever reason, she sent no messages.

He was beginning to wonder if something else happened after the trial, something his mother wouldn't tell him about. Of course, the trial itself would have been quite enough to drive Ariella away, and he did not blame her in the least for leaving. But now he had to find her, make sure she was safe.

He had recruited some of his friends, the young noblemen who sometimes visited him, to help him drug the guards. He succeeded in tempting the guards to drink some excellent wine, and when they fell asleep, he made it as far as the city gate before he was seized.

Some of the good citizens recognized him, and mocked him as he was led through the city.

"It's the prince who doesn't want to get married!" they called.

"Maybe he doesn't know what to do with a wife?"

The crowd roared with laughter.

"I'll teach you what to do, Your Highness," a woman shouted. "It's not that bad."

Demetrius ignored them. He would have gladly endured even more taunts if it meant even a small chance of escape.

Next, he tried making a rope out of his bedsheets and climbing out the window, but was caught immediately as he reached the ground below.

He even threatened to kill himself, but the queen called his bluff.

"I know you want to live, to get to her."

Demetrius fell asleep each night nearly crying with

frustration. He came to realize he was powerless to escape.

And since he was powerless to escape, he began to use more subtle tactics.

"I was thinking of throwing a small feast," he said to his mother on one of her many visits.

Demetrius knew that the irony of his imprisonment was not lost on her. After so many years of slavery, here he was, a prisoner once again. Therefore, she tried to assuage her guilt by allowing him any comforts or luxuries he desired in his isolation, often making suggestions herself.

Since he could not be allowed a real sword, wooden swords and even instructors were provided for him to practice. Prized books or ancient scrolls he wanted to read appeared promptly in his chamber. Any food he desired was brought at once.

Even now, he was enjoying a hundred-year-old wine that had been kept for some official occasion, but he had used up almost the entire bottle in one evening. Demetrius lounged on his bed, glass in hand, while his mother sat soberly in an armchair.

"A feast, what a splendid idea!" she said. "Of course, you would have to make a certain promise if you wish to leave your chamber and use the feasting hall."

"I was thinking I could have a smaller feast in here."

"This is some sort of half-baked escape plan, is it?" the queen asked.

"I wouldn't dream of escaping, not when my own dear mother wants me here, close to her loving bosom."

"Stop your buffoonery." She stood up sharply and was about to leave, but Demetrius hurried to block her way to the door.

"I will stop, if you let me have my feast," he pleaded, "And I promise I will not use it to try to escape. I will give you my word as a gentleman."

"Though no doubt there is some other plot you're hatching," said the queen.

"Plot? Not at all. I simply wish to enjoy the company of a few young ladies before I'm forcibly married."

"This is the first I've heard you speak of agreeing to the marriage..." his mother said, looking pensive.

"I suppose you'll find a way to make me do it eventually. Starve me until I consent to do it perhaps?"

"That's a very tempting thought. But I won't go that far. Nor will I allow you this feast, however. It is probably meant to try to drive Edoline away by making her jealous. Is that what your ill-conceived scheme is?"

"If it's so ill-concieved, why worry about it? Why not allow a poor prisoner a little bit of joy in his miserable life? I tell you, mother, even in my days of slavery, I had more amusements at hand than I have here now."

Her lips trembled a little. She frowned and headed for the door. Demetrius never thought his mother was capable of crying, but he knew now he was wrong. Not wishing anyone, even her own son, to see her as anything but a strong ruler, she was leaving in order to hide her feelings. He was sure of it.

Without turning around she said softly, "You can have your feast."

Demetrius took pains to plan it. He asked the guards their opinions about the best looking young ladies, and he chose only twelve ladies of noble birth, convivial disposition, and beautiful appearance. He wrote the invitations in his own hand and asked the imperturbable servant to deliver them. From his friends, who were allowed to visit only if the guards were in the chamber watching them, he learned that the feast was already making quite a stir at court.

Just as Demetrius had hoped, it was not going to be a quiet affair, and Edoline would be sure to hear news of it. When the young women arrived, he almost forgot about his plan. For a moment, he was dazzled. They entered all at once. Their smiles, their beautiful dresses, the sound of their laughter transformed the dreary chamber of his confinement, despite the imposing presence of four guards, who were there to make sure no one passed him any instruments of escape. A few ladies hung back shyly, but most of them greeted him in a cheery and good-humored way.

"You Highness, why did you wait so long to invite us?"

"Your Highness, are you lonely here all by yourself?"

"Will you be free soon, Your Highness? How do spend your time here?"

They were charming, but he was not tempted by a single one of them. The face of his lady forever locked in the treasure chest of his mind, these could not compare. However, a little flirtation was part of the plan, and he had to admit it wouldn't be completely unenjoyable.

"Ladies, ladies, please. One question at a time. I spend my time quite drearily, I admit. Why did I not think to invite you earlier indeed? I was a fool."

"But what have you been doing here, all alone?" a particularly bold maiden asked. She had pert brown eyes and a slightly long nose that only increased her unique beauty.

"You really wish to know?" he asked.

"Of course!" the others cried.

"I've been reading the ancient histories. Did you know my ancestors, the kings of Sylcadia used to marry several women at a time? It's not the custom any longer, unfortunately, but perhaps I should revive it."

The ladies laughed. "Your Highness, you are quite naughty," a shy, round-faced girl standing in the back spoke up. Lady Elana, he thought her name was.

"I will show you another thing I've been doing," he continued. "But do sit down. There is wine and food for you at the table."

The ladies did not wait upon ceremony. They commenced feasting, while watching their host with curiosity.

"I am not allowed real swords, so these wooden ones will have to do."

He performed some impressive twirling of the two wooden swords, then picked up a third one and juggled all three. Thanks to the high ceiling of his chamber, he was able to throw them quite high, and he had developed a good level of dexterity during his imprisonment. The swords spun in the air, and he caught each one without fail. The ladies cheered.

"Thank you, thank you." He bowed and joined them at the table, taking a seat between the shy Lady Elana and a talkative young woman with jet-black hair.

Time flew by, and soon three of the ladies were playfighting with the wooden swords, another two were embracing and kissing each other. A few more were singing and dancing on the table.

Demetrius glanced at the male guards who were clearly enjoying the spectacle, as he was himself. He lazed in an armchair, sipping his wine, while the formerly shy Lady Elana sat in his lap and talked about how much she hated arranged matches, and that her mother was forcing her into one too.

"Well, we must resist," he said. "Duty is one thing, but living a life of unhappiness is too high a price."

"I agree," said Elana.

"So, everyone knows why I'm being held here, and they still mock me?" he asked.

"Oh no, Your Highness," she said earnestly, "We know you love that lady of Dezearre. And you have all our sympathies."

Demetrius smiled and brought her hand to his lips.

"Thank you for coming here today."

At this moment he had almost forgotten why he had planned this evening and was simply enjoying the company, but then he heard Edoline's voice at the door.

"I don't care if I wasn't invited," she was saying.

The others hadn't noticed it yet because of the racket they were making, but Demetrius knew her voice so well.

"I am his fiancee, and if you don't let me in you will answer to the queen!"

The door burst open, and Edoline appeared. A few of the other ladies noticed her arrival and bowed, but most went on with their festivities.

For a moment, Demetrius felt guilty. She had been his friend, and maybe still could be, though he would find it hard to forgive her for putting Ariella on trial.

Demetrius feigned complete nonchalance. Elana made to get up from his lap, but he put his arm around her waist to stop her. "Please, do not get up for the sake of my future bride."

Edoline looked beyond furious. It was almost too easy to manipulate her.

"What is going on here?" she shouted.

The guests finally realized what was happening and fell silent. The women who had been dancing on the table climbed down and were about to leave.

"I pray you, don't go," Demetrius said in commanding tones. "Duchess Edoline is the one who should leave."

"I am not leaving," Edoline said. "What is all this?"

"Oh, the ladies? I may have given them a little too much wine. My guards are right, though. I didn't invite you."

"So, you planned this whole evening to snub me?"

"Not at all, my dear. I just want to enjoy the company of my friends before you put an end to my happiness."

"You're drunk and talking nonsense," she fired back.

"I may be drunk, but I was in full posession of my faculties when I planned this feast, and I specifically remember I did not invite you."

"I see what you're doing," she smirked, "It won't work. I can never be angry with you."

"I thought I could never be angry with you either," he countered. "But now, you persecuted Ariella."

"I didn't persecute her. All I did was show her what future she can expect with you. Do you know the truth about your lady from Dezearre? She saw us that day, the day you fell ill. She saw us kiss. And she fled, filled with jealousy."

Demetrius sat transfixed as her words hit home.

"You planned that?" he asked.

"Yes, I wanted her to see it. But there is the difference between her and I. She can never forgive you, but I love you too much to let such things get in the way. I don't care if you kissed other women, I don't care if you kissed her or did other things with her. I will always love you, and I know we're meant to be together."

Demetrius was livid. He realized why he had not heard from Ariella. He realized his mother had lied to him about Ariella's whereabouts.

"I did do other things, many things," he said, maintaining his relaxed appearance, "Why, in this very bed."

Edoline looked pained for a brief moment before putting on a brave face again.

"You're only saying that because you wish to get out of this marriage," she declared. "Well, if marrying me is such a punishment, then let us get married as soon as possible."

Demetrius heaved a sigh as she stormed out. But for the moment, he was not very upset at the failure of his scheme. At least he had learned something new, and knowing about all of Edoline's scheming he would feel a lot less guilty about escaping the marriage.

"Well, ladies," he said, "that did not go as I planned, but then nothing ever does. Who wants more wine?"

CHAPTER 12

Ariella was in a daze, but she was still cognizant of being taken into a small back room. A weasely looking man who sometimes served as a makeshift physician now arrived and poured some pungent liquid into her mouth. Soon everthing felt far removed. The pain still racked her body, but at the same time it seemed elsewhere.

The weasely man bandaged her broken leg. She didn't trust his skill, and didn't feel as if he had properly put the bones back together.

Tazain's voice was saying something, insistent.

Eventually she realized he was encouraging people to bid. To bid on her? Suddenly the room was filled with other people. But why would he want to sell her now, when she had come out the winner?

"Why?" was the only word her bloodied lips formed.

For the first time ever, Tazain looked contrite. "I'm sorry, I lost a lot of money in this fight..."

"You bet against me?" she cried in outrage.

"I mean, that woman with her hammer, she destroyed everything. Who knew you stood a chance? Anyway, I have to sell you at a loss, with your injury and all."

Ariella didn't know whether she ought to fear being sold to

someone else. At least in Tazain's service she knew what to expect.

On the other hand, it occurred to her that nothing could be much worse than this underground existence punctuated with bouts of fighting. And if he couldn't sell her, Tazain would probably throw her out in the streets anyway rather than take a chance on whether she could fight again or not and waste money on her food and medicine.

Her face probably looked mutilated beyond recognition. This would already devalue her as far as Tazain was concerned.

Meanwhile, there were not many takers. She could hear men's and women's voices discussing the offer but was too exhausted to turn her head and look at them. Then the weasely man bandaged up her face, and she could hardly see at all.

"She was good, bus she looks half dead," a man said, "I don't know if she'll be able to fight again. Maybe I could still use her as a laborer. I'll give you a hundred rals for her."

"Nonsense," Tazain insisted, "You see, she will be patched up soon. She fought well, and she'll fight again."

"What you're trying to sell us here is your refuse," another man piped up, "You expect us to take her and pay for her recovery? What kind of fools do you think we are?"

"I'm offering you a good slave. It's just that I need money quickly."

Ariella felt sick. She didn't know if it was from the pain, the drug, or this talk. To lose consciousness would have been an enormous relief, but she was wide awake, though she tried to close her eyes and block out everything around her.

"I will make a bid," another voice said.

It was a familiar voice, but she could not quite place it.

"Ah, there's a man who knows good female flesh when he sees it!" Tazain said brightly.

"I offer two hundred," said the familiar voice.

"Sir, you insult me. And I thought you were well versed in slaves."

"Fortunately for you, I'm not."

Ariella craned her neck to try to see who it was through the narrow slit between her bandages. A man wearing an extravagant hat so his face was shaded, but she could see something familiar about his appearance.

Even if she could recognize him, she tried not to let on. Tazain would surely raise the price even more if he knew they were acquainted and the buyer had a real interest in her.

"You know, I originally bought her for eight hundred," Tazain boasted.

"What would you do with a fighter, Vidor?" one of the women asked, "Combat is not exactly your type of business."

"You never know, I might try something different."

Of course, Ariella thought. It was the innkeeper. She didn't know what he was doing in these parts, but she felt a stirring of hope. He was a tricky fellow and probably wouldn't buy her only out of the kindness of his heart, but he was not altogether a miscreant.

"I will give you three hundred," Vidor said.

"That's highway robbery."

"All right then, four hundred and that's my last bid."

"Sold!" Tazain cried at once, probably afraid of losing the only interested customer.

Ariella knew she was somewhat safe, and she lapsed into a nightmarish sleep filled with blood and torture. There was a familiar figure in the dream, and she knew it was her enemy, Theodos. She could only see the outline of a shadowy form, but she was sure it was him.

When she awoke, she was resting on something very comfortable. A real bed, perhaps. And there was sunlight. The nightmare of Tazain's cages was over.

A soft, round face loomed over her, a woman's face she did not recognize.

"She's awake now," the woman said to someone in the back of the room.

Vidor came forward, and Ariella could have hugged him except she did not feel up to moving any part of her body. Her face still felt like it had been cut in half. She was still racked with exhaustion and pain, although it was not as completely devastating as it had been. They must have cleaned her up too because her skin felt somehow less encrusted with dirt. She also realized she had no clothes on beneath the blanket, but then it was nothing Vidor hadn't seen before. It was a relief to be free of the filthy clothes she had worn in the fighting cages.

"I patched up your face," Vidor said, "and your leg. My father was a healer, and I learned a great deal from him. I hope you don't mind, I think there are no good physicians in these parts, no one who could have done a better job than me."

"Thank you," Ariella said, "They would have thrown me out into the streets if it hadn't been for you. I wouldn't have lasted long."

"Think nothing of it, my lady."

"But Vidor, there must be something you want from me."

He nearly hopped up and down with excitement, and she knew he was dying to tell her something.

"Ah.You may be right, but this is not the time to discuss it. You need rest."

"I don't know if I can take part in your theater anymore. My body, my face... completely mangled."

"It's not that bad, love," the woman said.

Vidor shook his head.

"It's not that, or at least not in the way you did before. Do not fret. When you're feeling better, I will make you the offer, and you'll be free to refuse if you wish. Although I purchased you, I do not by any means intend to keep you as a slave. What I have in mind, you must agree to of your own free will. But I think it's something that could benefit both of us. Rest now. Gisele will watch over you."

Ariella was going to ask if Gisele was one of Vidor's actresses, but it took quite an effort to speak, and he was already off. She got a sort of answer when the woman bent over her and planted a soft kiss on her lips. She had never been kissed by such incredibly soft, plump, pillowy lips before, Ariella thought before she passed into unconsciousness again.

***

Three travelers on elven steeds provided an interesting sight, even to the wordly populace of the fabled city of Argentz. It was quite rare to see elves on their fabulous steeds in those parts, and Mara was somewhat pleased to find herself and her companions marveled at.

"We will go straight to the palace," she told her friends, "We can enjoy the delights of the city later, if there's time."

Her two companions seemed to be hardly listening. They gaped at the street vendors, the children, the buildings with as much fascination as the people who gaped back at them.

"But if they've locked your friend Demetrius away, they wouldn't likely let us speak with him, would they?" Lorel questioned.

"I know," said Mara, "but something tells me we have to go to the palace anyway, if only to be polite and pay our respects."

"Maybe they'll lock us up," Evoe said excitedly, "Then we'll walk right through the walls and escape! That'll give 'em something to think about."

"You two could," Mara said, "but I couldn't."

"You could do it too, Mara," Evoe insisted.

She laughed and shook her head. "Have you forgotten I'm human, not an elf?"

"I'll bet you never thought you could have visions of things far away, but you do now."

"Anyway, they're not going to lock us up."

"How can you be so sure?" Lorel asked. "From what I hear, that's how humans work. You do the slightest thing wrong, they put you in prison. They've even put their own son in prison."

"You can't get cheeky with them, Mara," Evoe advised.

"We'll see," Mara said. "I make no promises."

Surprisingly, they were admitted to see the monarchs quite soon after their arrival. Mara was on her best behaviour, and the king and queen were very gracious with her. Even Lorel and Evoe refrained from gaping or other strange behaviors, trying to look dignified as they represented the elf kingdom.

At the foot of the throne, they bowed, and Mara began her speech.

"Your Majesty Queen Larissana, Your Majesty King Gaufridus. I come from the Ringing Woods, and King Larkos sends you his regards. My companions are Evoe and Lorel. We came here to speak with Prince Demetrius."

"We have never before received an ambassador from the elf lands," the king said, "and we are most gratified. Please give your King Larkos our highest regards."

"However," the queen interjected, "we cannot not allow you to speak with Prince Demetrius, for he is unwell and not in a fit state to see anyone."

"How do you know my son?" King Gaufridus asked.

"We met on the road leading to the elf lands," Mara said, "He was very kind to me. He took me along when no one else would and brought me to the Ringing Woods. And so I found the elves who have welcomed me and accepted me as one of their own."

"You must tell us more. Please dine with us this evening," said the king, though the queen looked uncomfortable. "Your companions also. I have never met the elves of Ringing Woods, and I hope this will be the beginning of a new friendship."

The royal dinner was amazing. Evoe and Lorel tried to learn table manners as they went, while Mara spoke with the king about her adventures. She told him everything, not trying to conceal the fact that she had been a beggar and a thief when she first met Demetrius and Ariella. With her visions, she had seen how often people lied, and she began to understand that clarity and truth were not just abstract virtues but powerful forces without which all was darkness.

The king was impressed with her tale, but still they were not allowed to see Demetrius.

Mara had known this avenue would fail, but at the same time for some reason she was glad she had tried. The next stage of her plan was to seek some of Ariella's allies. She knew some of them had traveled here with her, and she began by asking in all the taverns whether anyone knew of a group of people from Dezearre that had arrived somewhat recently. Evoe and Lorel enjoyed every moment. They were fascinated by being given food and drink in exchange for money, which was not a practice of the elves.

The food was at times delicious and other times awful. In either case, the two elf siblings rejoiced. They listened to anything people told them with great interest, even if it had nothing to do with their search.

After a few days of fruitless conversations, a barmaid told them of a woman from Dezearre who had established herself as a good physician and lived nearby. This was the first lead they had, so they headed to the address they were given.

As soon as they entered the small quiet chamber that smelled of herbs, Mara knew she was in the right place. A tall, black haired woman had her back turned to them as she mixed some ingredients in a bowl.

"What can I do for you my dear... elves," she said somewhat shocked as she turned to face them.

Instantly Mara was hit with visions. First, she saw this woman in her younger years at the top of a mountain, engulfed by a fierce snow storm, praying to the gods. Then, the same woman inside the walls of a castle with a baby in her arms. There were flowers all around, and it was a peaceful scene. Somehow Mara knew this woman was not the mother, but she loved the baby all the same.

"You've made a long journey," Mara pronounced, "and yet you might have to make another one. My name is Mara."

"I know that name," the woman said. "I heard you were lost in the Ringing Woods, but now you're back. Ariella told me about you. I'm Jaquelle."

CHAPTER 13

The next day, Ariella had recovered well enough to get out of bed and move about on crutches, which Vidor had provided. She hobbled down stairs onto the main floor of the Three Brolougs, a very humble establishment but a popular one. Although she felt a bit conspicuous, with most of her face bandaged up and her leg in a splint, she was impatient to hear Vidor's proposal, and they sat in a quiet nook over a cup of Koroi whisky.

"May I ask you something?" Vidor began.

"Of course, anything for the man who saved me. I truly mean that."

"I saw the fight," Vidor said. "You didn't have to suffer a broken leg. You had the advantage there at the end. Why did you not defend yourself at that moment?"

Ariella stared intensely into her drink.

"I wanted to be sure of killing her. I had the opportunity then, and I didn't know if I would have it again. But more importantly, I'm finished defending myself."

"Now, that is an interesting philosophy. What brought it about?"

Ariella threw back the fiery liquid, and it almost instantly seemed to dull the pain of her injuries.

She leaned back in her chair, trying to formulate an explanation to something she had not completely fathomed herself.

"I suppose you could say I tend to react strongly to things. That's what brought me here, to the borderlands. I was hurt and wanted to defend myself against the world. I wanted to leave everything behind. My friends, my enemies, even my name. You may have heard, I am known as Cashain here. And that way I probably thought nothing could ever hurt me again. But during that fight, I realized that the time for defence is over. I found the will to attack again. And now I will keep attacking, for there are a great many enemies I must deal with."

"I am glad to have caught you in that mood," Vidor said.

"You need me to fight someone?"

"You see, I have a problem. I try to stage my plays here, thinking I had found the perfect place. You have vagabonds, outcasts, mercenaries living on the brink of civilization. You would think they would be a wonderful audience, and they are, save for one man who has decided to make my life a living hell. He's offended by my plays, you see. According to him, the gods are offended, but what does he know of the gods? Anyway, he has ruined more than one performance, threatening my actors, sending his men to chase them off the stage. He destroyed my decorations, and my beautiful Gisele nearly got hurt."

"Who is this man?" Ariella asked.

"His name is Howell. He thinks he is the big Toroi around these parts."

"I had a feeling."

"You know him?"

"We've met. And I can't wait to meet him again, this time with a sword in my hand."

"What I propose is this: we take over the town."

Of all the things he could have said, Ariella did not expect that. But the more she thought about it, the more the idea appealed to her.

"I've been waiting for an opportunity like this," Vidor

continued, "to find a warrior who is not only skilled but also inspiring. I wouldn't dare go up against Howell with anything less. When I saw you fighting in that cage, I knew it was meant to be."

"How would we do it?" she asked.

"In the same way as Howell has, but better. He owns part of everything, from what I've learned, but we'll do one up on him. We intimidate everyone, buy up everything, have enough fighters to support us if needed. Your 'faithful dog' reputation will put us in good stead with the people around these parts. You will lead the warriors, of course. In short, we will basically dictate the law, and then I could do my plays in peace."

Ariella grinned, then winced with pain. Her injured face was not ready for such merriment.

"All of that, just so you could do your plays?"

"Of course. My plays are important to me."

"Fair enough. How many fighters do you currently have?"

"Four. And that's barely enough to protect my actors."

"And definitely not enough to take over Nor Kemur. So... how do you propose to get more?"

"I have funds. Your friend the elf king was more than generous."

"My friend..."

"I don't suppose you know, we had the pleasure of meeting."

She looked up at Vidor in fascination.

"But you told us to avoid the elf forest on pain of death! And yet you've met the elf king?"

"I hardly had any choice after the so-called King Theodos burned down my inn."

"What? That little bastard. Now I have another reason to kill him... wait, this isn't on account of my staying there, is it?"

"There are probably a thousand reasons why he did it," Vidor said.

"No, I owe you a debt, Vidor. And even if I didn't, I would still want to help you with your new... venture."

"Good," he said, his blue eyes glinting.

"I have some debts to settle with Howell myself. As for the so-called King Theodos, we'll get to him later."

"Revenge takes money, everything takes money," Vidor said. "But once we've established ourselves here, we'll also be making more money through my plays and other enterprises."

"One thing, though: no slaves."

"Agreed. I was never an admirer of that particular trade."

"When do we start?"

"As soon as you're better. Your leg should heal in four weeks or so."

"Four weeks?! Right now that sounds like a lifetime. Can't you do something? Your father was a healer, you say?"

"I don't know... I could try to think of something. Meanwhile, I'll purchase a sword for you."

Despite Gisele's continued assurances that it was not too bad, Ariella thought her face was completely disfigured. She looked at the reflection in her new two-handed sword. A huge scar ran down her forehead and cheek. Vidor had promised to remove the stitching soon, but even so she did not think it would look much better.

Still, she felt it made sense to carry the scar as a memento of that encounter. She had killed someone who had done nothing to her, while the people who badly needed killing were still alive. Ever since that death match, impatience ate away at her. The time of her recovery seemed to crawl by. She had regained her ability to feel, and mostly what she felt was rage.

Meanwhile, Vidor worked a miracle. He obtained a tough resin from a rare tree to stiffen the bandages on her leg. He removed the splint and put the bandages with the reddish substance on her leg instead to hold it perfectly immobile. After a week of bed rest, he allowed her to walk for longer periods and even encouraged her to put weight on the broken leg to keep the muscles active.

Although it was a nuisance in all other ways, her broken leg was quite useful in playing the role Vidor had written for her in one of his plays: the victim of a massacre.

Ariella was not exactly thrilled at playing a victim, but after all Vidor had done for her, she wanted to do him a good turn.

She was nervous for the first performance. However, she comforted herself with the thought that this time she would only be on stage for a minute or two, and would be clothed. This particular play also would be less scandalous than the ones Vidor held in the private rooms. It would be performed on a moveable stage set up in the middle of the inn's main floor so that the regular customers could view it. But the actors would not be completely disrobed and would only perform suggestive acts without going all the way.

The tables were decked out in long, grey tablecloths especially for the performance to match the decor on the stage. There were shiny grey swaths of fabric representing luxurious chambers, and the actors were all dressed in antique costumes.

Ariella didn't know whether the rough and ready audience appreciated all of these artistic touches. They were already spilling drinks all over the tablecloths while fondling bar maids. At least everyone seemed to be getting into the spirit of the play.

Ariella sat alone until her cue. The leading actor, a tall, dark-haired fellow with a fine body but a face too brutish looking for her taste, paced back and forth until another actor said: "News from Scythia, a messenger comes with ill tidings."

Ariella hobbled onto the stage on her crutches, pronouncing dramatically, "They are all dead. Dead! Slain by the evil tyrant. And he is coming for you next Theopraxis."

"Then I shall meet him in battle!" the actor playing the hero cried.

"Do not go, my dear, it is much too dangerous," an actress dressed in a revealing nightgown begged. "No doubt it is a trap."

"I care not if it is a trap." the hero said courageously.

"I will do anything to keep you from harm," said the heroine. "Even... give in to your desires."

She began to kiss him passionately. Ariella tottered back to her table, casting a look at Vidor. He nodded in approval.

Just as the couple on the stage began to do some serious petting of each other, a troop of armed mercenaries with Howell in the lead burst into the inn. His massive physique and his arrogant demeanour made Howell difficult to ignore even when he wasn't surrounded by armed fighters. Now, all attention was on him instead of the play.

Seeing him again made her hands clutch involuntarily into fists. She felt like a trapped animal, despite being surrounded by allies.

"You didn't learn your lesson the last time," Howell pronounced. "You will now. I'll put an end to your shameless displays."

He strode towards the stage, drawing his sword. The leading actress fled but the actor who played the hero confronted him, pulling a sword hidden beneath the decorations. The rest of Howell's fighters, fifteen or so, headed straight for Vidor, who stood behind the bar.

"Now!" Vidor commanded.

Every audience member dropped to the floor and whipped their crossbows from beneath the long tablecloths that concealed them.

Ariella had a throwing knife ready. From her position at her table, she was facing Howell almost head on. But as she was about to throw, he looked directly at her and recognition made him pause. He turned instinctively away. The knife found its mark, but only in Howell's upper arm.

It was barely enough to slow him down. He looked around, to find most of his men shot down by crossbow bolts. The actor advanced towards him menacingly.

Howell pulled the knife from his own arm with barely a grimace, and without even trying to throw it back at his assailant, fled from the room. It happened so quickly that none of Vidor's men thought to stop him.

Ariella never imagined Howell would run. She was in a panic.

"Catch him! Catch Howell!" she and Vidor both shouted.

Ariella hastened outside as quickly as she could without falling over on her crutches. Vidor's warriors ran on ahead, nearly colliding with each other in the doorway.

She was blinded by sunlight as she emerged from the inn. Glancing around wildly, she saw no sign of Howell. Warriors ran down both directions of the street while Vidor joined her.

"Might as well wait here," he said.

"If he got away, he will be back with more troops," she said grimly.

But to her relief, soon a crowd of warriors approached, leading Howell before them. He was unarmed, goaded onwards by their sword points.

Ariella stepped into the middle of the street. She put on a pair of gloves she had prepared for this, with metal protection on the knuckles and of course, to give her punches more of an edge. Howell tried to run past her, but she stuck out a crutch that caught his foot and tripped him. A few people laughed, but most were gravely silent. A sense of impending death hovered over the scene.

Howell struggled up and tried to run, but was cut off by Vidor's people. He was now surrounded and looking around wildly for an exit but finding none.

"Uh... shall we kill him?" Vidor asked, standing at a safe distance.

Ariella agreed, but she did not want too quick an ending. "Kill him? No, I must thank him. He helped me a great deal."

In a way, she meant some of what she said. It was Howell's doing that had brought her to that fighting cage, where for the first time since leaving Sylcadia, she had regained the will to live, the fury of a true fighter, and the thirst for revenge.

She came forward to face Howell.

"I thought you wanted to teach me a lesson," she taunted, raising her fists and dropping the crutches.

"What's this?" Howell said disdainfully, "I will not fight a crippled woman."

"You had no compunction about fighting a tied-up woman. Maybe you think it's not chivalrous? But wait, didn't somebody once tell me chivalry could get you killed around here?"

She threw a punch, and it thudded into his jaw. He stumbled back then turned to flee, but Vidor's bodyguards pushed him back towards Ariella.

She punched low this time, just below his chest. Howell collapsed, completely winded.

Ariella did not wait for him to get up. She hobbled over and kicked him hard in the ribs, satisfied to hear Howell's grunt of pain. She walked around him, enjoying the sight of her fallen enemy.

"You were right about me, you know," she said pensively, "I didn't think the borderlands could touch me. Well, now they have touched me, and I have touched them."

He got up painfully and suddenly struck with his fist. The sudden, explosive blow connected with her temple, then another one came at her cheekbone and Ariella fell over, her bad leg giving way easily.

She rolled and was up on her feet again, though somewhat unsteady. She barely felt the pain of the blows, completely consumed with her vengeance.

"I don't have your gift for reading people," she continued, "So, I don't know what made you such a scoundrel. Did your mother not love you? Did your sweetheart leave you for someone else? Actually, I don't care."

Howell panted, clutching his sore ribcage. He made to punch her again, but she ducked. All her anger exploded, and she no longer had any taunting words, only attacks that she unleashed on her opponent.

She stopped to breathe when she realized his whole face was bloodied, and he was about to fall over. But Howell was nowhere near defeated. Suddenly he lunged towards one of the warriors nearby, surprising the man and knocking him down with a low tackle. Both fell to the ground, but Howell rolled to his feet again and, having thus broken through the deadly circle, took off at a run.

Ariella was about to order her fighters to give pursuit, but the twang of a loosened crossbow startled her.

Howell fell to his knees, a bolt in his back, another in his throat. Vidor must have given the order wordlessly to one of his loyal men.

She made her way to what was practically a dead body, wheezing its last breaths. Vidor stood beside her, looking down.

"I'm sorry," he said, "you probably wanted to kill him yourself but I couldn't afford to let an enemy live."

Ariella shrugged. "It seems your lack of chivalry killed him. Too bad he won't live to appreciate the irony."

"Well, that all went more or less as planned," Vidor remarked. "Shall we finish off the day by freeing some slaves?"

"Absolutely."

They had planned it all together. The first part had been to lure Howell onto their territory by staging the play. The second part was a bold attack on Tazain's cages in broad daylight. Tazain was always well-protected and surrounded by guards, but even he would not think anyone would suddenly invade his establishment with an army of mercenaries.

"To the cages!" Ariella commanded.

The fighters were so excited that most of them ran on ahead, forgetting that she could not keep up. Vidor gallantly handed her the crutches and stayed by her side, along with his four loyal men who formed a protective barrier around them as they made their way towards the building that housed the cage fighting arena.

"We really must work on their discipline," Vidor remarked. "But I suppose I'm happy, as long as they have enthusiasm..."

Tazain's stronghold had fallen by the time they arrived at the hall with the iron cage. Vidor's warriors had subdued or killed all the guards and secured Tazain in their firm grip. At this hour of the afternoon, there had been few customers, and those that were there fled for their lives, leaving nothing but a mess of empty tables covered in food scraps and half-empty glasses. The foul odour of sweat and despair still hung about the place just like she remembered. The smell of food which also wafted in the air made it even worse.

"Take everything I have!" the half-dwarf begged, "Take the slaves, the gold, everything."

"We fully intend to," Vidor assured him.

Tazain's eye fell on Ariella.

"Cashain, you're an honorable warrior. You wouldn't kill me in cold blood."

Ariella was silent. She could not believe he expected any mercy from her, but then again, he was simply frantic with fear.

"I treated you well, I gave you food and shelter," he continued.

"A woman died here," Ariella said, "and I killed her to entertain people, to make you rich. And now her life must be repaid... but not in gold."

A noise from the other side of the hall alerted her. All the liberated slaves emerged, eager to see their captor get his just rewards. In the light of day, they looked even more bedraggled and filthy. Ariella realized she must have looked the same not so long ago.

"Kill him! Kill the wretch!" they cried. "Or let me do it!" Each woman was clamoring to be given the chance to to take revenge on their tormentor.

"It should be Gerta," Penelope's bass voice cut across them all. "She's been here the longest."

Gerta stepped forward from the crowd. She looked exhausted and filthy, with red shadows under her eyes, but the eyes themselves were lit up with fierce happiness.

"Good to see you're still alive," Ariella said.

"You too."

"Take my sword."

"Give him a sword as well," Gerta gestured at the pitiful former slave owner. "Let's put him in the cage."

Ariella nodded, and the warrior obeyed.

Even with a sword in his hand, Tazain did not look much more threatening. With Gerta standing between him and the cage exit, he tried to get around her and break free. But she did not want to play cat and mouse games. She advanced on him, and he looked too terrified to fight properly. A few weak parries punctuated by whimpers were all he could muster. Ariella nearly turned away in disgust, but she wanted to see how it ended.

Gerta backed him up against the cage wall. He was done for.

A swish of the sword, a gush of blood, and his sword arm dropped to the ground, cut off from the elbow.

A shrill, wordless scream was the only sound that filled the hall.

Gerta paused, probably to relish the sound. He screamed for quite a while, but eventually quieted down to mere whimpers.

"All right, you've cut off my arm," he whined, "You've made me pay for what I did to you. Now spare my life. I beg—"

He never finished the sentence, for Gerta plunged the sword into his chest. More hideous screams ensued. She had to stab him several times before he fell silent.

The killing was horrible, more like an execution than a fair fight, but Ariella had wanted it done for Magdelne, that bitter woman whose spirit might rest easier if she were avenged.

In the ensuing silence, she began to speak.

"This marks the end of slavery in Nor Kemur. Vidor and I will make sure the rest of the slave owners either free their captives and leave this town or meet a similar fate. All of you who have been confined here are free to go where you will. But if you have any interest in joining me..."

"Yes, Cashain, we're with you," said a deep voice. To her surprise, it was Penelope.

"I'm definitely with you," Gerta agreed, leaning tiredly on the sword.

"We're with you!" the other women took up the call. "We're with you!"

***

The morning after the feast, Demetrius got up blearily but nevertheless decided not to indulge in more sleep. The new information he had received made him anxious to do something. He had been working on filing away one of the bed posts with a kitchen knife in order to create a club with which he could fight the guards. He was reluctant to do so because attacking his own people seemed wrong, but desperation drove him to keep working on this flawed plan.

After a couple of hours, he was almost there. The wooden post collapsed, bouncing a few times on the soft bed. At this exact moment, his father entered the chamber.

"Not giving up," the king remarked, "I like that."

Demetrius breathed out a deep sigh. His father was certainly more sympathetic to his plight than his mother was, but whatever his opinion of his son's imprisonment, he tacitly supported her. Demetrius collapsed onto the bed, feeling completely drained. He looked up briefly and noted that the king was wearing his sword, which was fairly unusual.

"To what do I owe this pleasure?" he asked.

"We had a visitor," Gaufridus said, "Someone who wanted to speak with you. She said you had met in the elf lands. Mara was her name."

"Mara!" Demetrius stood up at once and came over to his father. "I would like to see her. Is there any way I could?"

His father smiled mysteriously. "I think we may be able to arrange that."

He unbuckled his sword belt and handed it to Demetrius saying, "Here, it is yours now."

Demetrius was too stunned to speak.

"When Mara and her elf companions came here yesterday," the king continued, "it made me see how many strange and life-changing experiences you must have had on that journey, not to mention all the intervening years in Chaldea. It is no wonder you are so different from the boy who left us all those years ago. It would be foolish to expect otherwise, and it would not be fair to you. Your mother should accept it, and maybe one day she will."

"Father, thank you for understanding."

Demetrius hardly dared to hope that he was being released, but he put the sword belt around his waist.

"It looks good on you," the king said, his voice quavering slightly with emotion. "Now go. Your mother is in a council session and will be for two or three hours. I have released the guards from their duties."

"But mother will kill you," Demetrius exclaimed, "No, I cannot leave like this for fear what she might do to you."

The king smiled and shook his head.

"She will be angry at first, but she won't kill me. She loves me. I am as sure of it as I am of the beating of my own heart. And I want the same thing for you."

Demetrius was overcome with feelings. He rushed to embrace his father.

"Thank you, father, thank you. I'm sorry we couldn't have more time together."

"So am I. But I don't believe the gods are so cruel that we shall never see each other again."

"It won't be easy to get past the guards at the city gate, but with this sword I stand a chance."

"I ordered all the guards to let you through. I think you will find people around here still tend to obey their king," he said with a wink, "Now hurry."

After bidding goodbye, Demetrius rushed from the chamber, sorrow at leaving his parents mixing with a heady brew of hope.

His father must have ensured that there were no other guards around because Demetrius made his way out of the palace without incident. He wasted no time and headed for Emelote's quarters in the city. Surely, she would know something of Ariella's whereabouts.

CHAPTER 14

Like all of Vidor's ideas it seemed insane, yet it began to work.

Maybe it was the ruthless efficiency with which they had removed their rivals, or maybe Ariella and her new army's formidable reputation, but no one sought to upset the balance of power again. The queen's magistrate, who was officially in charge of the town, appreciated the bribes he received from its new rulers. A sort of peace reigned over Nor Kemur.

With the gold and riches they had seized from Tazain, they made investments in the wine trade and also bought two of the most frequented inns, the Sprightly Pig, and the Three Brolougs. Of course, these places had plenty of rooms for both private and public plays.

Vidor was even jollier than usual these days.

Ariella could tell it was not so much the prestige and the power of his new position that appealed to him. It was just the freedom to be left alone to work on his beloved business. And he had made sure of doing so by seizing control of the town. There was a sort of logic to it.

Although there had been rumours at first that she and Vidor were lovers, these soon died down as Vidor was often spotted leaving his actors' quarters in a rather disheveled state.

He favored both male and female actors and seemed to have a special fondness for a blond young man called Xanthus, who had recently rejoined the troop, having been separated from them by King Theodos' raid on Vidor's former inn. But as far as Ariella could see, Vidor's greatest passion was his art, the business of writing and staging the plays.

Surrounded by the lasciviousness of the theatrical performances, Ariella could not help but have certain thoughts, which were however not directed at any one person. She tried to keep that side of her life secret, especially from Vidor, who was much too curious.

They feasted in one of the private rooms where the 'real' plays took place. A smaller audience who had paid a hefty sum for the privelege, watched the actors' unclothed antics. By now, Ariella's face had healed and the bandages on her leg had been removed. She still walked with a slight limp because of the weakened muscles, but she felt less conspicuous appearing in public, and although the scar was still there, a long line down the side of her face, it was not as horrible as she had feared.

The play was about two men who loved the same lady and then decided to share her affections.

They had just reached the point where Nia, the beautiful dark-haired actress began to disrobe to prevent the men from fighting over her. She untied the laces of her dress and as it fell to the floor the audience breathed a lustful sigh when they saw she was wearing nothing at all underneath. Her black hair flowed over large, firm breasts. The hair around her sex was shaved, revealing everything.

Vidor chose this moment to whisper in Ariella's ear.

"You know, Gisele is mad about you. I think you won her over with your heroics. She nearly fainted when you were carried from that fighting cage."

Although Ariella had not thought about women in that way, she relished the memory of that kiss for its novelty and tenderness. "Oh yes, she kissed me with her soft, pillowy lips. It was wonderful."

She could not help but stare as Nia kissed each of the male

actors, and they were now undressing too.

"Well?..." Vidor prompted.

Like everyone else in Nor Kemur, it seemed he was keen to learn why she had no interest in men, nor women for that matter. Ariella tried to evade as best she could.

"It's only that... these actors depend on us for their livelihood. It would not be fair to lie with them. Some of them might agree to do it, feeling as if they had no choice in the matter."

"I assure you the ones that lie with me do so of their free will."

"Of course, I meant no offence. You're an attractive fellow." She punched him playfully.

This was not mere flattery. Although Vidor was not classically handsome, his contagious energy and his intellectual prowess were bound to win him some admirers.

"Ah, my lady," Vidor said rubbing his shoulder. "only you would think of honor and justice in a place like this, practically a brothel."

"If it was up to you, the whole world would be a giant brothel."

"That would be fine indeed."

"And yet, this a place of art as well," she pointed out.

"I would hardly call it art," Vidor made a dismissive gesture. "I parody the great writers, nothing more."

"Your parodies are quite good, though. I wouldn't be surprised if you had a play of your own waiting to spring forth from your imagination."

"I am honored that you think so."

The dark-haired actor called Roan was now embracing Nia from behind and fondling her breasts, while the blond actor, Xanthus, caressed her pubic area and began to stroke inside her with his fingers. Her moans of pleasure were only a source of frustration to Ariella.

"We are friends are we not?" Vidor asked.

Ariella had not even thought about it, but it didn't take her long to decide that strangely, they were.

"I suppose we are."

"May I ask something?"

"Well, yes. Now you have me curious," she said.

Now, Nia was down on all fours, pleasuring Xanthus with her mouth as he kneeled before her, while the other man thrust into her from behind. Their moaning was so loud, Ariella did not worry about her conversation being overheard.

"When we first met, that man you were with... and I do not say this in a covetous way... but he was the handsomest man I had ever seen, and your act that night was probably one of the best performances I've staged, unrehearsed as it was. Where is he now?"

Ariella sighed. She had wondered sometimes whether Demetrius was looking for her, or whether he had slowly resigned himself to his fate. But surely he could have talked to Jaquelle or Emelote by now and figured out her whereabouts. He would have been here, if he really wanted to. As she watched the actors doing unspeakable things, her blood coursed faster, but she was never attracted to any one of them. Even thinking about touching the handsomest of the men caused revulsion.

"That is a long story..." she said. "We had to part ways. And speaking of honor and justice, I had to leave him behind because honor demanded it."

She heaved a deep sigh again, but then she grinned. "Trying to ensure your safety, eh? By reminding me that we're friends?"

"No, well yes, maybe," he conceded, "But what I meant was, I care about you as a friend, and I want you to be happy."

"I'll be happy when Queen Esclairmonde is dead."

She speared a muckpitt as if it was the queen and ate it off the blade of her knife.

Maybe it was from that conversation that her new name originated.

Shonrok. The Bride of Death.

She fancied this one less than Cashain since she didn't like people speculating about whose bride she was, even if it was Death. But if it intimidated her enemies, so much the better.

Of course, some were more intimidated than others. A fairly rough and ready fellow named Aucon, who was officially a guard working for the magistrate, a frequent visitor to Vidor's shows, and probably a robber in his spare time, seemed to act more and more boldly each time he visited their establishment. Ariella wondered if he was possibly a spy for Queen Esclairmonde. No one here knew her real name, but she might be recognized by description, and the queen would surely not have given up trying to kill her.

The final provocation happened during a particularly brilliant performance of The Remoares and the Giotos, a classic tale which Vidor saw fit to rewrite in his own inimitable style. Instead of the bloodbath of the final act, the two feuding families made peace by engaging in a lavish orgy. Because this performance took place in the public hall, the orgy was only pretend, but its lustful dance was enough to make the audience of drunken thieves and mercenaries cheer.

Ariella sat with Vidor and Giselse at their usual table when Aucon came swaggering towards them.

"Enjoying the show?" he sneered.

"In fact, I am," she replied.

"It sickens me," he began, "seeing you sitting on all this wealth and not even using it. You drink little, you eat little, and you bed none of your 'actors' or anyone else, as if your female parts were touched by a frost monster."

There was ominous muttering all around. Although all had gossiped about her lack of company, no one dared say it in her face. Ariella did not erupt into anger, for she thought the metaphor was amusing and rather apt.

"And if they were," she said, "what business is it of yours?"

"Simply that it sickens me, and I will not stand for it. It's time for a new leader."

"So you wish to take my place, do you?"

"I wish it, and I shall."

"Then you'll be happy to know there is one sort of pleasure I have not forsaken."

She stood up and swiftly drew her sword.

"Not in here, please," Vidor said at once. "Don't forget we own this place."

"I will respect your wishes, Vidor," she assented, then turned to Aucon, "Outside you shall answer for your impertinence."

Chairs scraped against floorboards. The actors froze in their evocative poses. No one wanted to miss the fight.

Ariella still walked with a limp but it did not affect her fighting very much. She had been practicing with Roan, one of the actors, who was quite a good swordsman.

A short and wiry fellow, Aucon did not look imposing, but he was dangerous with a sword, everyone knew that.

Ariella squinted in the sunlight, letting her eyes adjust.

"I could use the exercise," she said to Vidor, who held her cloak for her. "Things have been going so well for us I've gotten a little too comfortable."

She had her two-handed sword. It was not the same one as had been passed down in her family, but it would do just as fine a job at slicing through this rude fellow.

"Are you ready?" she said carelessly.

Aucon's reply was to attack. Vidor sprang out of the way, and Ariella easily blocked the first thrust.

He attacked even more aggressively, but she was fast enough to parry or evade each stab or slash. Something had changed in her after that battle with Magdelne. It had been an incredible victory after so many defeats. Now, her star was ascending in the night sky, and she felt stronger each day. Aucon was not much of a challenge, but she decided to draw the fight out a little for the sake of amusement.

She changed tactics and suddenly lunged at him. He was equal to the challenge and riposted almost instantly.

But suddenly Ariella was distracted by the chittering of a glider somewhere behind her. She dared a glance and saw the distincive figure of someone approaching. Having looked away, she nearly got run through as Aucon tried to take advantage of the momentary lapse. Ariella stepped aside from the thrust, right after she stole another incredulous look at a woman coming towards her. A short, slender woman who nevertheless looked imposing in her elven attire, with her majestic walk and reddish golden hair, the small, squirrel-like creature sitting on her shoulder.

In three strokes the battle ended.

Ariella circled around her opponent, grabbed his arm in a painful lock, and seized his sword out of his grasp. Before anyone could blink, she was holding both swords crossed against his neck.

"Do you still wish to take my place?" she asked.

"No, no!" Aucon stumbled backwards, but she did not pursue him.

"Thank your lucky stars, you are spared this day," she said quickly, then sheathing her own sword and throwing Aucon's to one of her followers, she turned back towards the woman who approached.

"Mara!"

There were whispers all around, "The Bride of Death has a friend?" "Maybe this is her long-lost lover." "It's an elf!"

Ariella didn't care. She ran towards the new arrival and enveloped her slender body in a crushing hug. Mara responded in kind with her willowy but surprisingly strong arms. The glider squeaked happily, leapt onto Ariella's shoulder and snuggled in her hair.

"Mara, you're well again?" Ariella asked, though she could see no trace of the former madness. It was hard to believe such a miraculous recovery.

"I'm more than well."

"I hope you'll stay a while? Stay as long as you want, really."

"I'm sorry there's not time to explain," Mara said, "but we must ride out at once. All your people, including Jaquelle, are being held by the Koroi. Demetrius is with them too."

This news made her heartbeat surge, moving her into action.

She beckoned Vidor over.

"Is that Mara?" he exclaimed.

"Yes, it's me. Don't worry, I won't steal none of your

trinkets," she said, sounding very much like her previous incarnation.

"Such is life," Vidor remarked philosophically, "You think you've left your traveling companions behind... but they may just be waiting for you at another crossroads."

"Vidor," Ariella spoke in low tones, "I'm going to have to bargain with the Koroi chief. I'll need to take some of our provisions, if you don't mind."

"Of course, half of it is yours anyway. But why the rush?"

"People who are important to me have been captured."

"Then take some of the bodyguards as well."

She thought this over. "Thanks, I hope it won't come to a fight. He has thousands of troops up there. But I may need some people to guard the supplies. And I'll take quite a bit of gold to exchange for the prisoners."

"Then I'll help you get ready," Vidor said.

He was off, giving the orders secretly to his trusted guards, not wanting news of a gold transport to get around.

Meanwhile, Mara introduced her two elven companions, who stood a ways back.

"It's our first visit to the human world," Lorel volunteered.

"It's a cesspool, isn't it?" Ariella said.

"We love it!" they exclaimed heartily.

Ariella laughed. "I've missed the company of elves."

She approached one of the horses and stroked its grey flank. It was the most graceful animal she had ever seen, with a long, delicate neck, a beautiful head more like that of a sea horse than an actual horse, and lean but strong legs.

"You have ridden long, and your mounts must be exhausted. Let me find you some new horses."

"No, they are hardier than they look," Lorel said proudly. "They need the exercise, though we've been through quite an adventure already."

As they saddled their horses and waited for the gold and other supplies, Mara recounted how she found Jaquelle and Emelote, and then was joined by Demetrius, who had just escaped from being imprisoned by his mother.

"His mother kept him imprisoned?" Ariella exclaimed, while tightening the girth of her own mount. "Well, of course she did."

"That's right, but he couldn't wait to get to you, the poor thing," Mara said, "So we fled the city as quickly as we could, fearing that the sky would fall on our heads if the queen was to catch us. We were all set to find you, and Emelote told us that the last time she met with you, you spoke of the borderlands. We also had the glider you used, and were fairly sure it was leading us in the right direction. Then who would catch up to us but Duchess Edoline with a horde of her troops? She was practically foaming at the mouth with rage that her fiance should run away from her."

Ariella felt a strange sense of satisfaction. So Demetrius had chosen her over Edoline in quite a demonstrative way.

"And she thought to try and bring him back by force?" she asked.

"Actually, she wanted to kill him," Mara said.

"Poor Edoline. I don't blame her."

"Well, she wanted to fight him anyways, even though he tried to evade combat and refused to attack her. But it didn't matter because just in that moment, the Koroi descended on us in swarms. Evoe, Lorel, and me were the only ones who escaped. We used our elven abilities to go invisible."

"I always knew Mara could do it," Evoe said.

"I lost my mind but got something in return." Mara looked proud.

Ariella was suddenly reminded of that night in the Ringing Woods when she had promised the elf king she would consider his offer if she ever saw Mara alive and well again. And now that time had come. Larkos had made good on his promise.

Larkos could be trusted, and she had felt a magnetic attraction to his elven beauty. But she could not think about it now. She wanted to save her people, even if it included saving Demetrius and Edoline as well.

"Edoline is with them too?" she asked.

"Yes, she got captured along with everyone," Mara replied.

"And I do believe she's the only one who deserved it."

"Oh gods," Ariella implored, "give me the strength to do the right thing."

They rode through the midday heat along with Gerta, Penelope and a few other loyal guards. Mara and her companions led the way, although Ariella could have probably found the encampment herself, for she was fairly certain it was the same one where she had been held captive. The ride took about two hours, but felt eternal.

At last, there were the two hills by the side of a small stream, and there the tents of the Koroi. A group of riders approached them at once with forbidding frowns and drawn swords.

"Let us not draw our weapons," Ariella said to her company, "At least for now."

"Who are you?" one of the Koroi riders shouted.

"It's Cashain, or Shonrok as they call me now. I wish to speak to Riobard at once."

News of her and Vidor's takeover of Nor Kemur must have spread here. The guards considered their group with more respect if not with less distrust.

"I will report to Riobard," the man said, "Wait here."

Just as she expected, they were admitted very quickly inside the camp. As she rode through the circles of tents, suddenly she felt short of breath at the thought of seeing Demetrius again. Though she was not sure whether it was that or fear that he had already been killed or sold off as a slave, sent somewhere she could never find him.

Riobard himself emerged from a nearby tent and greeted them.

"Cashain! The gods had not deceived me. But it's Shonrok now, the Bride of Death, isn't it? Either way, I knew we'd meet again."

He was not as drunk now as the last time they talked, and

he looked genuinely pleased to see her. She suddenly realized that if the thought of closeness with a man had not been repulsive to her, she would have deemed him attractive.

"Riobard," she began, "I come to you with an offer of trade."

"Good," he said, "We shall talk it over as we watch some of these captives being punished."

She felt her knees go weak. But she forced herself to smile and walk along with the chieftain as he led her towards a raised platform.

"Please, sit with me," he said, inviting her up to the highest level, which looked comfortable, laden with cushions. "Your people may sit below."

Ariella nodded to the rest of her company, and they took the lower seats, glaring around them with distrust. Only Mara and the elves looked serene.

"You see, this man tried to escape," Riobard said, "killing Shilong, who was my friend, my best warrior."

Ariella was glad she was sitting down. The man he pointed to was Demetrius. Her breath caught in her throat when she saw him down below being led towards the platform by two guards.

"What is it?" Riobard asked with concern.

"Just some dust," she lied, coughing convincingly. She could not let Riobard know how much she cared about saving this particular prisoner, or he would demand the moon and the stars. He might even wish to trade Demetrius' life in exchange for the others. Ariella could not allow that; she resolved to free them all, make sure none of them were harmed.

Demetrius was ever the same as she remembered, though a slight growth of beard shaded his face and a few scratches lined his upper body and his arms. He was stripped down to the waist, every muscle gleaming in the sun. She recognized the spark of humor in his blue eyes and knew he was ready to mock the proceedings.

As he approached the platform, Demetrius looked astounded for a moment, but then promptly lowered his eyes after seeing her.

He bowed. "Beautiful lady, and... honorable lord," he began.

"Silence, you wretch," Riobard commanded. "You will now pay the price for killing my best warrior. Our law demands it. If you are brave, you will die well and we will bury you with all appropriate honors."

"You will make my fiancee very happy," Demetrius replied.

"Begin," said the chief.

Ariella had to act quickly. She now estimated their chances of escaping with all the prisoners to be zero. There were simply too many of them to convey from the camp, which was swarming with thousands of Koroi warriors. She had to win this by diplomacy. She had to get to the heart of the matter quickly but without sounding desperate.

"I'm sorry about your fallen warrior," she said, "But would you do a kindness for me and spare this captive? Punish him if you like, but spare his life. He's one of my followers, and I will pay you handsomely for his return."

"So this is why you've come?" Riobard said, looking pleased with himself. "Then we truly have something to bargain for."

"Your other captives too, they are all my people."

"Actually, they are now mine," he corrected.

He motioned to his attendant and ordered to bring out the rest of the prisoners. Ariella had not quite believed they were all here, but her amazed eyes beheld Jaquelle, Emelote, and about twenty of her former followers, ones she thought had abandoned her and gone elsewhere to seek their fortune. And there was Edoline with a number of people who must have been her personal guard. They were all led into the circlar space in the center of the tents, surrounded by a semi-circle of Koroi spectators on either side of the platform on which she and Riobard sat. For now, it did not seem any of the other captives were in danger, but the two wooden beams stuck in the ground in the center looked suspiciously sinister. She tried to read Riobard's face and saw nothing but decisiveness in his dark features.

Demetrius was led up to the two heavy wooden beams, his arms tied to them.

A man with a big whip set to his task at once. Demetrius tried not to flinch or cry out, and all they could hear were muffled grunts as his muscular body winced with each stroke.

She turned to Riobard.

"We brought a thousand Rals in silver and gold, as well as some newly-forged swords. They're yours, just release the prisoners."

Riobard yawned as if he was bored with both the spectacle and the conversation.

"That's all very well," he said, "but you already know what I really want, Shonrok. You weren't willing to give in, even when the other option was slavery."

"You mean to ride into Dezearre under your command?"

He nodded.

She steeled her face not to look sympathetic as she directed her gaze at the grounds. The whip continued to snap, its rhythm getting faster. Demetrius still did not cry out, but blood began to trickle down his back.

Ariella had thought she would be indifferent to his fate, but now she realized just how wrong she was. Despite everything she had suffered, despite feeling that she no longer loved him, she could not bear to see him hurt. She resolved not to look, but to work on persuading Riobard.

"What about the money?" she asked, "I thought you needed that too. I recall you mentioning how few traders would deal with you. There was Howell, sorry about killing him by the way, but now that he's gone, Vidor and I could replace him as your trading partners."

The chieftain smirked. "You are a warrior, Shonrok, not a merchant."

He beckoned one of his men forward and gave him some instructions. In a moment, the man returned, bearing Ariella's sword and the pouch with the magic crystal.

"As a sign of good will, I give you these," Riobard said.

Her heart nearly burst with excitement at seeing these items, which she thought were lost to her forever.

"They were mine to begin with," she pointed out, "but thanks."

She tried not to look too long at what was happening below but could not resist. She thought there would have been a part of her that liked to see him suffer, but even if there was, it was so small that it made no difference in her pain on his behalf.

For a brief moment, she thought she could see a faint smile on his lips. He had either found something else that was funny or he was glad to be able to display his courage for her in this stoic act.

"He's a brave man, I like him," Riobard said, "A pity I'll have to kill him because you're not willing to pay the price. And he won't enjoy the next part."

"What's the next part?" she couldn't help asking.

"Oh, it is a true test of bravery."

Demetrius was now untied from the two posts. He staggered over to the next place of torture, where he was placed with his back against a big, round wooden target. His wrists were thrust into iron brackets, securing him in place.

A group of archers took their positions at the other end of the grounds, closer to the audience.

"You're going to execute him?"

"Not so quickly. They will aim mostly around him, but perhaps some will try to make the smallest cuts without killing him to show off their skill."

"That is most cruel. Could you not dispense with this part?"

Riobard instead raised his hand commanding them to begin.

"There must be something important about this man if you will consider speaking with me about these matters when you previously refused."

"He's loyal to me and has served me well. Would you not do as much for your people?"

"If you were you tied up there, and he was up here with me,

what would he do?"

She didn't have to think hard; Demetrius would do anything to free her. Would he give in to all the chieftain's demands or run down to the grounds and shield her body with his?

Had Riobard somehow guessed this? Or was he merely suspecting it?

"Do you know the story of the drowning man?" Riobard asked, his shrewd eyes keen with hidden laughter. "The one who refused all the boats who came to rescue him? 'God will save me,' he insisted. And you know what happened to him..."

"And I'm the drowning man, am I?" Ariella smirked, "That story is so old it has a beard three feet long."

"And nevertheless, its meaning rings true. Would you really forgo this opportunity, just to spite me? Think of where your pride brought you before. And why did you first come here, to the borderlands? Because you must have believed in your heart of hearts that the Koroi were your way back into Dezearre."

"I just wish you weren't so obnoxious," Ariella blurted out.

The chieftain grinned.

A new idea sprang to mind. If Riobard wanted this conquest badly enough, he would yield to her wishes.

"We are in agreement then?" he asked.

There was no time to lose. The first arrows were flying. Ariella held her breath. Demetrius looked ahead at the archers, unflinching. The perfect features of his face were composed. The arrows struck the wooden target all around his body, not touching him except one that barely grazed his cheek.

"Almost," Ariella replied, "But there are three more conditions you must meet. If I ride with you, your warriors will not harm any of the common people. This war will be waged in a chivalrous way. No burning of villages, no torturing, no killing of peasants. We will meet their armies in the fields or lay siege to their castles if need be, but we will not harm the people of Dezearre. Especially not if you wish to rule over those people."

The archers aimed again and arrows flew.

169

She glanced down and saw Demetrius wince with pain, though he made no sound except a hissing breath as an arrow cut deep into his arm.

To her relief, Riobard nodded. "Very well. I might as well begin to act in accordance with your northern chivalry, even if your own kings and queens never do."

"Two, Queen Esclairmonde is mine, for I have sworn vengeance on her."

"Agreed, as long as you dispose of the vixen. What condition are you saving for last? I wager I won't like it."

"I will be in command," Ariella said looking unflinchingly into his eyes.

She did not read utter contempt in them. It was a good start.

"I'll need time to think," he said.

"And you're talking to me about pride? Do you think you can become the first Koroi king in the Northern Coast without sacrifice?"

"King of the Northern Coast," he corrected.

Ariella shook her head.

"Dezearre is mine, but you will have your own kingdom if you help me."

"A big chunk of land?" he asked.

"Obviously."

"As big as Dezearre? Good land, not rocky crags or anything like that."

"Of course," she said hurriedly, "My word is good."

He stroked his chin pensively, but his eyebrows were drawn together.

"I still need time to think."

The archers were aiming their next volley.

"No time," Ariella insisted, looking down to the grounds, "if he dies, this negotiation is over."

She could not risk any more arrows being let loose. She offered her hand. Riobard suddenly broke into a grin and shook it.

He shouted something in the Koroi language to his men,

and the archers let the their bow strings relax. Two men were dispatched to untie Demetrius. They held him up to prevent him from collapsing as they led him away. Other warriors were already cutting the ropes holding the prisoners.

"One more condition," Riobard said.

"What is it?"

He pointed to Edoline.

"That woman... I get to keep her."

Was her lucky star smiling down on her at last? This was too good to be true. It would be a huge relief to have Edoline out of the way. The duchess must have found out something about her affair with Demetrius to make her this angry. If it was true that Edoline had tried to kill her own beloved fiancé, then what would the enraged duchess try to do to her?

Still, Edoline had not really done anything to her yet, and now that Ariella had time to reflect, she was the one who had come unbidden into Edoline's life and upset her engagement. At least she could make sure Edoline would not be harmed.

"Why do you want her?" she asked.

Riobard smiled mysteriously. "If you won't reveal your reasons, I don't have to reveal mine."

"You remember what you said about making a pet of a broloug?"

"You think I don't follow my own advice?"

"Well?"

"If there's one thing I hate doing is making a fool of myself. The woman will ride under my banners. She will be safe, much safer here than in your den of debauchery."

"Done," Ariella said at once.

Riobard commanded for Edoline to be taken away, and Ariella felt slightly guilty for enjoying her rival's screams of outrage as all the other prisoners were freed except her.

"Though she won't be riding with you very long," she mused, "not unless she's had some lessons in swordplay since our last encounter. If you want my advice, look to her training."

"Any advice from Shonrok is gratefully accepted," Riobard

said, standing up and making a respectful bow.

"You know," Ariella said, "I think we're going to get along."

CHAPTER 15

Ariella was pleased with the outcome, especially since Riobard invited her to a feast that evening and ordered one of his men to show her around the camp. Her knowledge of Koroi was a little rusty, but she spoke to the proud-looking warrior in his language, asking him to take her to the former prisoners. The tall, dark-eyed man whose name was Rushiao was not exactly impressed, but slightly less stand-offish.

They walked to a row of tents nearby, and Ariella ducked into one of them hoping to find Jaquelle.

"Just who I was looking for!" she exclaimed.

She then realized Demetrius was in there too, sitting on a pile of blankets, his whole upper body and his left arm tied up with bandages.

Jaquelle was just fastening the last of the bandages on his arm when she looked up. Demetrius tried to stand, but Jaquelle's hand and words stopped him.

"You need to rest. If you try to stand and undo all my work, I will kill you myself with a rusty spoon."

He sat back down, suppressing a smile. Despite her fierce words, to Ariella's astonishment, there was warmth in Jaquelle's way of addressing Demetrius, and he seemed fully at ease around Jaquelle.

Ariella came forward, trying to read Jaquelle's face, hoping for an embrace, and it was granted. As always, Jaquelle could not be angry with her for long.

"I'm sorry I left you, Jaquelle."

"Oh, nonsense. I think it was good for you to be on your own a while, though you just couldn't stay out of trouble," she said, pointing to Ariella's bad leg.

Her shrewd eye must have caught the slight limp.

"I was going to send for you and Emelote to join me, for all our people to join me when I was ready."

"I know. Now, you two should probably have your talk. I'll have a look at your face later, and your broken leg."

To her utter surprise, Jaquelle made to leave. Ariella tried to signal her to stay, but the older woman would have none of it.

"He came all this way to see you," she whispered emphatically, "Now talk to him."

Jaquelle left, and there he was. It was strange to see him again, just as alluring as ever. A little pale from his ordeal, and possibly as uneasy as she was, now that they were alone. She had rarely seen him look this nervous. He was trying to gauge her mood, just like he had done on their first meeting when he was still a slave.

"Ariella..." He was about to get up again.

"Stop!" she commanded, "didn't you hear Jaquelle? Sit down."

Despite her protest, he stood up, and she could see his impulse to hold her in his arms, but when he saw her dark look, he desisted.

"I see..." he began, "you're angry with me."

"Angry? That may be the biggest understatement I've ever heard."

"I know why you're angry," he said appeasingly. "But now that I've found you again, we can start afresh. When I saw you sitting there with the chief, I knew you would save me."

Despite her resolve to put up an emotional wall, she was touched.

"I thought I saw you smile when you were down there,"

she said, "What were you thinking about?"

"I was thinking how both you and Edoline probably would have loved to snatch the whip away from that fellow and do the job yourself."

"I knew you were thinking of something funny," she said, giving in to his charm for a moment. "It's true, I thought I would have loved to see you being tortured, but no. I found it unbearable. Because of how close we used to be."

"That scar..." he said, making her instantly conscious of her face. He did not seem to look at her with any less adoration for it. "I loathe myself for not having been there to help in your battles. Now, I will no longer leave your side."

"But you must understand, it is over."

His face growing even paler, he came closer despite her gestures of protest.

"Ariella... I love you," he said. His eyes pleaded for mercy. "I've never said it properly before, but I do. I'm sorry I have such a poor way of showing it, but I will try to do better."

In the past, she would have been indescribably happy to hear those words, but now that her heart had been embittered by all the humiliations and the travails their love had caused, there was only regret and scorn.

"You're too late."

"All right, you wish me to beg, and I will."

"No, I just wish you to leave. "

"Not this again... we've tried being apart, and it didn't work. We must either be together or at opposite ends of the earth, you said so yourself."

"Then I choose opposite ends of the earth."

"Why did you save me then?"

"I didn't want you to die, nor anyone else."

"You could have saved the others without saving me. But I knew you would, although you took your sweet time about it. You were probably just curious what I would look like riddled with arrows."

"I just want us both to live long, happy lives. Don't you understand, no love is worth so much pain and suffering."

"On the contrary," he said, "only love is."

His eyes looked into hers so honestly, and she knew he was sincere. She knew he had never intended to hurt her. But whether intentional or not, the damage had been done.

All that time when she was numb from the pain the affair had caused, unable to cry, unable to feel. She could not even begin to explain to him how much she had suffered and why she would never forgive him.

But at the same time she pitied him, standing there and offering her his heart, looking so defenceless.

"Love is not enough," she said more gently, "When I fled from your palace, all I had was some hope of regaining a shred of honor. And it's all I believe in now. We have both been selfish, putting ourselves before all others, before your kingdom. But now you if you wish to regain any kind of honor, you will marry Edoline, rule over your people, and forget about me."

His lips formed a hard line in response to her words.

"I can never forget you. And the marriage would be a lie. Is it what you really want, for me to live a lie?"

He came closer. His body was completely enthralling. Although he wasn't that much taller than her, he seemed to tower over her with his ripples of muscle concealed by tight bandages. She would give in to desire if he even so much as touched her hand.

"You must regain your health," she said, avoiding his gaze, "But in three days, you will leave. And in that time, I do not wish to see you or speak to you."

Before he had the chance to say another word, she stormed out of the tent.

However, Demetrius caught up and walked along with her.

"Will you stop that?" she yelled. "You will bleed out of your wounds."

"I care not."

She stopped walking and faced him. There were not many people about, and the Koroi probably did not speak their language. In any case, Ariella was too incensed to care who saw them arguing.

"Very well, you wish to explain?" she said, "To apologize maybe for what you did?"

"Yes, I do, though not all of it was my fault. What was I supposed to do? I wanted to keep you close to protect you, but by bringing you close, I rekindled the affair."

"It was not entirely your fault, no," she agreed, "But what happened after... I know Edoline planned it all, but you... you kissed her! Why did you do that?"

It was all she could do not to cry, the memory of it slamming back into her mind.

"I'm sorry you had to witness that. I needed to do it, to bring the whole thing with Edoline to an end, a proper end."

Ariella suddenly understood. She had never thought of it that way, but after years of yearning for Edoline, of course he would want to bring it to a close. The kiss did not mean that he chose Edoline. But her anger was not assuaged.

"It was still a betrayal of me, of everything we had."

"It was only a kiss. If you had wanted to kiss someone from your past to help you reach an ending, I would not be so troubled."

"Really? You would like it if I kissed another man?"

"I wouldn't like it. In fact, I would probably want to kill him, but it would not take away my love for you."

"Well, I haven't kissed anyone these past months because you've made all men repulsive to me," she shouted.

She felt the sting of unshed tears growing unbearable. Opening her eyes wide to let the liquid evaporate in the dry desert wind, she walked away as quickly as she could, and this time Demetrius did not follow.

Ariella was invited to feast with Riobard and was asked to bring her military commanders and advisors as well. She had no official leaders except Emelote, so she chose Gerta, Jaquelle, Mara and her elf friends as well to make for imposing numbers. Then she sent a few of her guards back to Nor

Kemur to let Vidor know that all was well. The Koroi feast would last well into the night, and she did not expect to return until the next day.

The feasting tent was a big circular structure lit brightly with oil lanterns. It felt inviting, and despite her past experience of being told all her life the Koroi were the enemy, fighting the Koroi and of being captured by them and sold into slavery, she trusted their leader. A few musicians played the trilling pipes of the Koroi accompanied by soft drumming. Riobard and his five military commanders bowed as the company entered, and Ariella and her people did the same.

Rushiao, the man who had helped her get her bearings in the camp was there too, along with three more Koroi commanders, all men, for the Koroi women hardly ever fought or sat in councils. She realized Riobard's sway over his people must be strong indeed to lead his tribe into forming such serious alliances with a party almost entirely comprised of women.

Riobard looked dignified, though she could detect some youthful excitement brewing beneath the surface. His certainty in the success of his conquest was contagious. Ariella had always believed it would be a fearsome enterprise, taking on Queen Esclairmonde, but Riobard made it seem like victory was already in their hands thanks to their alliance.

An elderly woman brought forth a big bronze goblet, and handed it to Ariella. She drank from it, the strong spirit of wildgrass burning her throat in a satisfying rush, then passed it to Riobard. He took a long swig.

"I, Riobard of Ruibai, son of the Great Toroi, declare my allegiance to you. I will fight by your side and treat you as one of my kin. If your horses lack water, I will let them drink before I drink. If an enemy blade threatens you, I will deflect it with my own sword. If victory is ours, we will share it as brethren."

Ariella repeated the oath. "I, Ariella, Baroness of Leduryon, declare my allegiance to you. I will fight by your side and treat you as one of my kin. If your horses lack water, I will let them drink before I drink. If an enemy blade threatens you, I will deflect it with my own sword. If victory is ours, we will share it as brethren."

"Our alliance is now sealed," Riobard declared. "Let us feast and forget about any wrongs we have done each other in the past."

Ariella and her company then sat on cushions placed all around the low table. The food was plentiful, and the drinking certainly helped ease any previous tensions or grudges either of them might have held. Ariella was out of practice, and the Koroi whisky went straight to her head, but it felt good.

After long months of abstaining from serious drinking, she knew that time was over. That woman who was always sober, always getting up at dawn and training for a fight every waking hour of the day wasn't her real self. She couldn't be that woman anymore. But neither was she quite her old self, the one who would drink herself into a stupor for the sake of momentary oblivion. And now that the wine flowed freely, she could drink it in friendship, not as a means to cover up her loneliness and pain.

Jaquelle spoke to Riobard's commanders of past battles, curious to know their ideas of warfare. Gerta gossiped about happenings in the borderlands with anyone who would listen, while Mara spoke to her elven companions, answering their queries about the Koroi.

They did not discuss strategy for the coming war, however, and Riobard mostly talked about how much his two brothers had annoyed him as a youngster.

"I trained with relentless effort just so I could one day beat them," he confided, "I suppose most boys learn to fight for the same reason."

"Evoe and I never fought," Lorel remarked, "that is what allowed us both to spend more time expanding our minds instead."

"I wish my brothers had been more like you," Riobard replied.

"Tell me something..." Ariella asked him, "Remember

when I fought you to protect the wagon? I threw a knife at you. How in all the realms did you manage to dodge it?"

"It's a matter of wisdom," he declared.

"Wisdom?"

"It is wise to avoid knives."

Mara and her friends laughed, while Ariella gave him a crooked smile.

"I see."

"I also have a question for you," Evoe addressed Riobard. "Do you think that if I stare for a long time at a blade of grass, both I and the blade of grass will be changed?"

"Of course," Riobard said without hesitation, "I believe the honorable Bai Meng mentioned something very much like this in his teachings, and I am a very devoted follower of his philosophy."

As evening darkened the tent and its surroundings, an elderly woman began to sing, accompanied by strains of the pipes.

Ariella thought it sounded somewhat like the songs Jaquelle used to sing to her when she was little. Sometimes not even Jaquelle knew the meaning of the words, but songs that were ancient enough sounded so much like many other ancient songs, even though they might have been sung in completely different languages.

The sad, slow melody was conveyed in an anguished voice with intonations that sounded like sobs and wails, but there was a feeling of something greater and more eternal than an individual person's grief. This overarching sense of infinite time and space seemed to allay the otherwise unbearable sadness.

"Do you know what the song is saying?" she asked Riobard.

"Yes, in fact I penned a translation of it myself. I hope to share many of these songs with your people when I am king in the Northern Coast."

"I should have known."

He spoke the words along with the woman's singing:

Tell me o gulls, have you seen my love?
The gulls said, we have flown the ocean wide
We have seen many miracles upon the tide
But we have never seen your love.

Tell me o gulls, will he look for me?
The gulls said, we don't know such things
We see the lightning and the rainbow's rings
But of the future we can't speak to thee.

Tell me o gulls, what shall I do?
The gulls said, do what your heart will
And so I followed their call so shrill
Forever journeying across the ocean blue.

"Lost love," Ariella mused, "People have always written songs about it, and probably always will."

"Unless someone finds a cure for love," Riobard said, "which is very doubtful."

Edoline waited a long time for anyone to come and bring her food and water. At last a woman did, but they did not speak the same language and she could not get any answers. Her hands were tied, and she was alone in the tent, but she did not have the resolve to attempt a solitary escape.

She was growing weary and hungry again, when the Koroi leader stumbled through the tent opening. Edoline had seen from their gestures as he and Ariella conversed earlier that he wanted to keep only her for himself. Why, she did not know, but she assumed the worst.

"What are you going to do, take me as a concubine?" she cried, straining desperately at her bonds, "Force me to marry you? Just try it, and I'll break all your ribs."

"I suppose that's what you expect of a barbarian like myself," the chief replied wistfully, "I really have to work on my reputation. But I assure you, I never have to force women to do anything. On the contrary sometimes they become too aggressive with me, and I have to flee their affections. I brought you some food."

Edoline relaxed long enough to stop pulling at her bindings, while Riobard put down a plate and a cup before her and settled onto the cushions a few feet away, giving her all the space she needed.

"Marriage..." he mused while Edoline devoured the meal. "I never even bed the same woman twice."

"Then you may soon run out of women."

He laughed. "It's not a problem I've considered... One day, I will take a wife. It is my duty as the leader of my people. But not anytime soon, not until I hold the Northern Coast."

"What vanity!" Edoline scoffed. "You're so sure you'll hold the Northern Coast."

"You may not believe it, and sometimes I don't believe it myself, but the gods have spoken to me. They said I would be a conqueror."

"Really. What else did they say?" Edoline queried, biting off a piece of meat.

"That I must ride with warrior women by my side. Only then will victory be mine."

"So that's why Ariella sold me to you... Well, I understand why she did it, to save everyone else, everyone she seems to care about but me, of course."

"I don't really understand whether any of you are friends or enemies," Roibard said, his eyes sparkling with humor, "Maybe one day you'll tell me what is between you two."

"I have been cruel and vicious to her," Edoline said, "but she deserved it."

"She is my ally, and I know it may rankle you, but you must help us in the coming fight."

"I must, did you say? No one forces me to do anything."

"I cannot force you, though you think I would try, savage barbarian that I am."

"Then wouldn't you rather have some gold instead? I'm a

high-born lady, and I will command a noble ransom. I'm sure you will need money for your campaign."

He shook his head. "I need you. My destiny can't be fulfilled without you."

"How do you know it's me, not some other woman who can fulfill your so-called destiny?"

His dark eyes looked wise beyond his years although she judged him to be no older than twenty-five.

"I just know."

"And you expect me to ride by your side into battle, when you're holding me prisoner. You expect me to help you fight alongside the woman I hate more than anyone in the world?"

"With time, maybe your anger will pass."

"Never!"

"Then you will never see your kingdom again."

Edoline was about to fly into a rage, but an intriguing thought stopped her.

"Are you saying that if I help you..."

"I will let you go," he said. "Once I have the Northern Coast, you'll be free. Now, I will untie you and hope you won't try to escape."

CHAPTER 16

The next morning brought a cloudy haze over the desert. Ariella had fallen asleep in her tent just as the first light of day was showing, and now, she was grateful for the slight softening of the sun's rays, but she did not regret the drinking of the previous night. It helped erase the feelings of anger against Demetrius, even though she still had no wish to see him. Her mind was now on the conquest ahead.

She met with Jaquelle, and they walked away from the main camp to sit on a hillside, where a little privacy and fresh air could be found while Jaquelle insisted on looking at her old injuries.

"Vidor set the leg and bandaged it," Ariella assured her, "and I wore the bandages for four weeks. It should be good."

"Well, you're still limping," the stubborn woman said.

Upon closer inspection of the leg, however, she seemed satisfied.

"This Vidor did a fine job," she said, "You just need to work the muscle more. The limp is only due to remaining weakness."

"Thank you for looking at it, anyway," Ariella said. She appreciated Jaquelle's care and fussing over her after so many weeks of absence.

"Now, that scar on your face... perhaps I could heal the

skin a little bit more."

"I think it's as healed as it will ever be."

"It wouldn't hurt to try," Jaquelle said, pulling the healing stones from her pouch. "A scarred look is fitting for a warrior, but not very good for a bride."

"A bride? Jaquelle, which magical realm are you in?"

"I just think Demetrius—"

"He had the chance to marry me," Ariella said, all her anger returning, "He did nothing but mope about and complain."

"Things were complicated then," Jaquelle said soothingly.

Ariella growled in frustration. "That was exactly what I said to you at the time. But you were against me. Why do you say the exact opposite thing now?"

Jaquelle was unperturbed.

"He has proven his sincerity. He escaped the palace and came here to look for you. Besides, he is quite charming."

Ariella could not believe what she was hearing.

"I see what's happening here. He got to you with his handsome blue eyes and his little jokes and his gentlemanly airs."

"Maybe if I were thirty years younger," Jaquelle said with a wink, "but I assure you my decisions are based of sound logic."

Ariella laughed. "There was never any sound logic about this whole situation."

Suddenly, Jaquelle took a more serious tone.

"I'm sorry if I have been a bad adviser. Things were complicated there, and I was too inflexible. Maybe you should have fought for his love, and I was of no help. I only told you what not to do at the time, but I gave you no better ideas or options."

"Well, it's not your fault," Ariella said. "I don't know if there were any good options."

Jaquelle worked on the scar a little while, and Ariella felt a slight tingle in her face as the crystals poured their energy into the wound. At last Jaquelle put down the healing stones and looked at the horizon.

"When I was a little younger than you are now, I was in a

similar place. I was so hard on you because I hated to see you repeat my mistakes."

Ariella held her breath. At last she might know why Jaquelle had never had a family.

"The village where I lived, far beyond the mountains, had many fine-looking men, but the one I fell in love with had newly arrived there... with his wife. I could not describe to you how much I loved him, and he loved me. I knew it from the moment we met. It was a madness. But at the time, it was the only thing I could think of, day and night. But all too soon, our affair was discovered. I was exiled, and what was more, his wife pursued me with a furious thirst for vengeance. She sent her servants to kill me, and I knew I wasn't safe unless I managed to flee to other lands. I decided to cross the mountains, and I chose a path so dangerous no one would dare follow.

"I prayed to the gods, and they heard my prayers. They led me to a cave to wait out the storm. I crossed the highest peak and came upon the Alchemist. He had been dwelling in these mountains for hundreds of years, and he gave me the crystal and taught me its powers. I knew then I had to seek you, and that my culpability would be atoned by the work I would do teaching you all the skills you needed."

"Did you never fall in love again?" Ariella asked, "I would feel terribly guilty if it was for my sake that you spent so much time apart from potential suitors."

Jaquelle shook her head. "I don't know if a love that strong can ever come within a single lifetime."

Ariella felt at peace, knowing things were right again between her and Jaquelle, better than they had been in many months, maybe years.

Next on her plan was to avoid Demetrius. Luckily, she had a good excuse. She needed to apprise Vidor of the new situation, so she rode back to Nor Kemur with a few guards, leaving word with Riobard that she would soon return to discuss their strategy for capturing the Northern Coast.

On returning to town, she found Vidor scribbling away at

one of his parchments in his study at the Sprightly Pig.

"I'm composing a new play," he said without looking behind him, "Whatever it is can wait."

"Even the invasion of the Northern Coast?" Ariella asked.

"Oh," he turned on hearing her voice, "I'll make an exception."

"No, finish your play," she said, "I need a drink anyway. I shall wait downstairs."

She got a bottle of beer to quell the slight uneasiness in her stomach from too many thoughts of Demetrius. Vidor joined her about half an hour later, looking proud.

"I have begun an original, not a parody."

"Good to hear!" Ariella said.

"As for that invasion, I'm with you."

"You mean in spirit, right?"

"No, I don't mean only in spirit. I would like to accompany you on your conquest. I recall a certain talk about taking revenge on our mutual enemy, a so-called king."

"Of course," Ariella said, pouring him a drink from the beer bottle, "though I expected you would allow me to take care of that. And I didn't know you were willing to leave behind everything we have built here."

Vidor drank the beer and sighed with satisfaction.

"Remember when you encouraged me to write my own plays? Well, this is you writing your own plays, as it were. And I would like to help you."

"Why? You owe me no allegiance."

"But I have the feeling my destiny is linked to yours, and if this small venture of ours is any sign of the success to come, then I will gladly join your cause. For too long, I thought I was only meant to live out in the margins, but now the time has come for me to be a true rebel, something that has always been my heart's dream, though I dared not name it."

"And you don't regret leaving your comfortable existence?"

"What we have built could easily be destroyed," he said, "even though our little empire here may appear more powerful than my previous enterprise, the inn, nothing is truly stable in this world."

"But surely we won't just abandon it? I would like for someone to stay behind and keep order, perhaps prevent the slave trade from taking hold again."

"So would I. And I believe some of the actors would be pleased to stay, not to mention some of the bodyguards."

"Good," Ariella said, "I am more than happy to have your help, Vidor. All we need to do is choose a few trusted people to take our place running this madhouse."

"I believe there will be no shortage of people not wanting to risk their lives attempting to depose the most powerful monarchs in the Northern Coast. Though you didn't tell me we have him on our side now!"

Ariella whipped around to see the person he was looking at.

Demetrius leaned against the doorway, taking in the scene. He must have been standing thus due to exhaustion from the long ride in his injured state, but he made it look most casual.

"Please, join us... sorry I still don't know your name," Vidor said.

"Demetrius."

"And he is not on our side," Ariella added, anxiety and anger making her short of breath. "He was supposed to marry Duchess Edoline and now she's here too, but I sold her to the Koroi. It's a muddle."

Vidor grimaced as he fought not to splutter his drink all over the table, but finally he swallowed it down.

"The prince of Sylcadia? And I made you perform in my theater. That was cheeky, even for me. I must apologize."

"No need, truly," Demetrius said, sitting down in a leisurely manner despite Ariella's glare. "It's good to see you, Vidor."

"Well," Vidor said, looking at his two companions at the table with incredulity, "since your matrimony is forestalled, you will surely join us on our campaign, Your Highness?"

"Join 'us'? I never took you for a military man, Vidor," Demetrius said.

"I am many things, and as our paths have crossed once again in a most fortuitous way, I took it as a sign that fortune favors the bold."

"Then I'll be happy to join you."

"How did you even find us?" Ariella asked.

"I speak a little Koroi. Your newfound allies told me where I might seek the Bride of Death. Quite an imposing title, though a trifle inaccurate since I am obviously not death personified, but I didn't want to make the announcement without your approval."

"I gave you three days to recover and leave our camp," Ariella said through gritted teeth, "Since you are obviously well enough to ride, you may leave immediately."

"It is not very fair to go back on your promise of three days' respite," Demetrius remarked, "I thought I might stay here for a little while and then accompany you back to the Koroi encampment."

"That was very presumptuous," Ariella said.

"Not at all," Vidor exclaimed, "The Sprightly Pig welcomes you. Take any room you like. We are rather short on customers at the moment."

It was now Vidor's turn to be glared at.

"It's just that the journey to the Koroi camp is dangerous," Demetrius continued, "I may need to be accompanied by some of your bodyguards."

"You may stay here," Ariella said, "but after we return to the Koroi camp, you will ride back to your kingdom as fast as your horse can carry you."

"Of course," he agreed a little too readily, which Ariella thought was suspicious. "If I may spend tomorrow night there and be gone in the morning..."

"It seems a fair agreement," Vidor said, while Ariella hesitated. She did not know why he wanted the extra time, but feared nothing good would come of it.

"Then I shall seek my room at once and leave you to discuss your business," Demetrius said. He seemed to realize he was pushing his luck.

"You didn't tell me he was here!" Vidor shouted in a whisper as soon as Demetrius headed upstairs.

"I was going to tell you. And why are you suddenly so enamored with royalty? I thought you couldn't stand them."

"Royalty generally strives to crush the common man, but Demetrius is a good fellow. Better to have a monarch on your side than against you. We need him. Why are you telling him to leave?"

"He does not even have the royal authority to command his troops, and in fact he hasn't brought any troops."

"Still... a single individual can sometimes do a great deal."

"I know that you mean well, Vidor," she said with a sigh, "but he had his chance to make things right. I fled to the borderlands leaving everything behind because my heart was broken, and I never, ever want to experience that again. Do you understand me?"

Vidor nodded. "I do not wish to suggest a path that would be against your better judgment," he said, "But beneath Epheor the sky there are many happenings that may seem unexpected and even unbelievable. One would think the prince of Sylcadia would have better things to do, but he has rejected his fiancee and come to the borderlands for your sake. He could have been married by now, but he is here."

"Well, soon he won't be here."

Vidor was silent for a few moments.

"I think he's up to something," he finally said.

"He's never up to something. He has the brains of a flea."

Still, she suspected Vidor was right. There was a certain carefree confidence with which Demetrius went about his business, and she did not like it.

When they rode back to the Koroi encampent with a few of her guards, she thought Demetrius would try to speak with her and defend his position once again, but he seemed to read her mood and deferred to her desire not to speak. He rode in the back of the cavalcade, letting a few other riders and clouds of dust provide a buffer between them.

A few glances she stole back at him revealed his decisive expression. He was certainly in pain from the wounds he had suffered; they could not have healed over night. But at the same time, they seemed hardly to matter to him. His jaw was set, his eyes seeing something beyond the arid landscape. This was not the look of a man resigned to his fate. Of course, she could not ask him directly what he intended to do, but now that he was obedient in keeping out of her way, she was tempted to talk to him. She spent the rest of the journey pushing these thoughts out of her mind and trying to focus on the coming conquest.

***

Demetrius had only one night to complete his plan. He would have to do it without much preparation, but perhaps that was for the best. As he rode among Ariella's guards, the sun burned as intensely as his desire for the angry warrior maiden. He was glad he made the journey to Nor Kemur, satisfied that she had no other lover there. But he realized by now that words would not convince her of his devotion. Only action could sway her.

When he was led away after being nearly shot full of arrows, despite the pain of his wounds, which tormented him even now, he had glanced back at the other prisoners to see what their fate would be. They were released, all except Edoline, who was led towards the eastern side of the camp. She disappeared among the tents, but at least Demetrius knew where to begin looking.

Later, after his talk with Ariella, he realized he had to do something bold to win her back. Saving Edoline from the clutches of the Koroi would be a good thing in itself, and might ignite her jealousy... He had wandered in a leisurely way among the tents on the eastern side, looking for a sign of where Edoline might be. One of the tents was guarded by two ferocious looking warriors, and he was fairly sure Edoline was inside. He became completely sure when he wandered around the place late at night after the feasting and saw Riobard himself enter the small tent.

Demetrius would not have hesitate to burst in there and kill the scoundrel if he heard any signs of a struggle, but the only sounds were of conversation, the words too muffled for him to hear. He waited in the shadow of another tent until Riobard left about an hour later.

He was prepared to rescue Edoline that very night. They arrived at the encampment in the late afternoon, and Demetrius rested until nightfall. He was tired, his back and his arm wracked with pain, but the physical suffering was almost forgotten in his excitement about his plan.

As the fires of the sentries began to crackle in the darkness, he made his way to Edoline's tent and softly called her name. There was not response. He had mostly done it to alert her, hoping that she would not utter any surprised exclamations when he sliced through the tent with his sword.

She must have been asleep, for when he entered through the opening he cut in the fabric, she rose up groggily. As soon as she saw him, she seemed to understand. She made no sound.

He was relieved to find that whatever anger Edoline had held against him was now gone. As their eyes met, she already silently agreed to his plan. She had the chance to escape, and she took it, following him out of the tent into the darkness beneath the starry sky.

CHAPTER 17

As evening fell, Ariella took refuge from the enigma of her former lover's behavior in the tent of the Koroi chieftain. At least Riobard seemed to be always well-disposed towards her and as eager as she was to begin their invasion.

However, they both understood the need for caution.

"In about thirty or forty days, the snow will melt on the hills of Dezearre," Riobard said as they sat over some drinks, "That will be the best time for us to strike, as my armies are not well-adapted to your winters."

"I would agree with you," Ariella said, "but for one thing: in that time Queen Esclairmonde's spies may sniff out our intentions. We would completely lose the element of surprise. Although, she may already know of my presence here."

She remembered her encounter with Aucon, who had not been seen since in Nor Kemur, and wondered if he was bearing news of her activities to the queen even as they spoke.

"Then let her await our coming," Riobard suggested, "Let her fear you."

Ariella gave this some thought. Perhaps he was right; sometimes letting the enemy wear herself down with endless worry was more powerful than any surprise attack.

One of Riobard's high-ranking warriors, a heavy-set man with a cruel look in his eyes, came over to the chief and whispered something in his ear. Ariella didn't know why, but this alarmed her.

Riobard left her alone in the tent, following his attendant outside. This was even more alarming. Usually, the chief treated her with the height of courtesy, but to leave so suddenly without telling her why meant something unprecedented had happened.

Not wanting to wait around for the bad news, she exited the tent, pushing the flap aside in impatience.

What she saw seemed utterly incomprehensible at first, until the heavy-set warrior said:

"We caught them trying to escape, Toroi. They were already a few miles from camp, heading back to Sylcadia."

A host of Koroi warriors were leading Demetrius and Edoline forward. At first Ariella could not fathom that they had tried to escape together. But Demetrius' behaviour, which had seemed strange at the time, now made sense. She could not blame him for wishing to escape and free Edoline since she herself had clearly rejected him.

The Koroi chief, however, blamed everyone.

She had never seen Riobard angry before, but suddenly it struck her that this was what it looked like. Trying to maintain an outward air of calm, he flared his nostrils, and his dark eyes turned to ice. He was absolutely livid, no matter how hard he tried to hide it.

"You dare betray me," he said softly.

Four of his men closed in on Ariella. They did not aim to capture her, perhaps not yet, but their crowding was uncomfortable. Steel rang as she drew her sword.

"Say plainly what you accuse me of," she shouted, "but keep in mind, I knew nothing of their escape."

The Koroi warriors drew their swords too, and Riobard did not stop them. He had yet to draw his, though his hand was clutching the hilt.

"You saved this man from his just punishment at a great cost," the chief said, pointing to Demetrius, "He is an esteemed follower of yours. Now, I find him trying to take the prize you had given to me to seal our alliance."

From his perspective, it certainly looked damning.

"He was not acting on my command," she said.

"Why should I believe that?"

Now Ariella found anger stirring within her chest. "Why would I do something so foolish as to break our alliance?"

"I intend to find out," Riobard replied, his voice almost a whisper.

"Ariella didn't know about it," Demetrius spoke in the Koroi language as he approached, goaded forth at sword point. "I acted alone in freeing Edoline. She is my fiancee."

Riobard at last relaxed his grip on his sword hilt.

"Is this true?" he asked Edoline.

"Yes," she said softly.

Although these words absolved Ariella, relief at saving the alliance was quickly replaced by more anger. To hear him speak of Edoline as his fiancee brought back all the worst memories of the royal palace in Sylcadia.

"I am sorry I doubted you, Ariella," Riobard said. He ordered his men to back away from her, and she put away her sword.

"I'm beginning to understand what is happening here," he continued, "And since your follower has acted against your wishes, you would not mind if I doled out a severe penalty for his reckless actions."

"Of course not," Ariella said, clenching her fist. "I would be happy to dole it out myself."

"No, please, spare him," Edoline suddenly said, "It was my fault. I convinced him to help me run away."

"Your sympathy for him does you credit," Riobard said. "You are brave to plead on his behalf, but he is the guilty one here."

"No!" Edoline yelled, straining against the guards who grabbed her.

"Fifty lashes, then," Riobard stated, "But no need to exert yourself, Ariella. My men will ensure he feels every one."

He was about to make a sign for the guards to take

Demetrius to the place of punishment, but Ariella preempted him.

"Surely not this very night? He hasn't recovered from the last time."

"He hasn't learned from the last time," Riobard argued. "You are strangely lenient. Do you not wish to punish him because he acted on your orders after all?"

"Of course I wish to punish him. But I believe it would be murder to whip him again."

"He may live, he may not. That is a chance we have to take."

"Give him a little time to recover, or make it twelve lashes only," Ariella suggested.

She faced Riobard's icy sternness once again. His face showed no vestige of compassion.

"Fifty lashes, tonight."

"Why don't you just fight me like a man?" a voice rang out, drowning out their argument, and Demetrius stepped forward to face the chief.

"Are you issuing a challenge?" Riobard asked. Suddenly his demeanor changed to one of surprise and interest.

The question was hardly necessarily, seeing the blue fire of Demetrius' eyes and his defiant stance. The guards moved to restrain him, but Riobard waved them away.

"You've captured me before with the might of your army," Demetrius said, "and you seem quite adept at giving orders, but I've never seen you wield a sword."

"I have," Ariella whispered to him urgently, "and he's very good. Don't do this."

"Then may I ask who am I to be a fighting?" Riobard demanded, "I'm the son of the Great Toroi. Are you worthy of crossing swords with me?"

He was obviously not so arrogant as to care about such matters, but he seemed curious if not desperate to know who exactly Demetrius was.

"Consider me a humble servant of the Baroness of Leduryon," Demetrius said.

"Is that all?"

"That is all," Demetrius said, "But rank means nothing when steel is drawn. I'm worthy of you in skill, and that is all that matters."

"To first blood, then," said the chieftain, "I would hate to die before my conquest of the Northern Coast has even begun."

"First blood," Demetrius nodded briefly.

This proclamation did little to ease Ariella's fears that one of them would kill the other as everyone gathered to watch them in the same level space where Demetrius had been nearly killed with arrows. First blood could be drawn with a deadly wound as well as a scratch, and the men faced each other with murderous fury burning in their eyes.

Koroi warriors and their women gathered, drawn by news of the duel which spread rapidly. The stars and the moon provided much light, but a few people also brought torches to illuminate the grounds.

"Give him back his sword," Riobard commanded, staring at his foe, "If you win, you may take the woman and leave. If I win, you will be whipped as many times as I like."

"Agreed," Demetrius said, stepping casually into a fighting stance.

Riobard rushed him at once with a fierce cry, but Demetrius only stepped a little to the left and evaded the brunt of the attack, letting his sword meet his foe's with a light parry.

"I hope you have good seamstresses to mend your clothes," he said, "for I will cut a hole through your fashionable vest."

"We have no seamstresses at all," Riobard replied, "We do not fear Sylcadian blades, which are as dull as your wits."

"Far be it from me to say something disparaging about the Koroi," Demetrius countered as he advanced, "You've already embarrassed yourselves quite enough in battles past."

Riobard was already enraged, so these words probably did little to pique him. Demetrius seemed to be taunting him mostly for his own amusement.

But soon, he was too occupied to think of new insults. The

Koroi chief slashed furiously at him, and Demetrius could barely defend himself. He was almost thrown off balance several times, but each time he achieved a desperate recovery.

Ariella watched as in a dream, feeling suddenly weak. For a moment, she imagined he was fighting for her. But that could not be. He had clearly chosen Edoline this time.

Her mind wanted Riobard to win. She needed him alive to complete the conquest, but she could not deny that her heart beat faster for Demetrius.

As she watched him fight, his long, dark hair flung about by the sudden movements of combat, his wicked grin flashing now and again even as he parried deadly strikes, desire made her breath quicken in spite of herself.

But he was clearly doomed to lose. A palace slave raised in luxury had no chance against a wild Koroi warrior who had been born and bred for the fight. She doubted even her own chances against Riobard. Even now, the Koroi chief was pushing him back with the fury of his attack.

Demetrius made one false step, tripping on a small rock that he couldn't see behind him. He fell, and Riobard stabbed down. Ariella gasped.

But already Demetrius had rolled away from the deadly blade. Riobard was not one to fight with chivalry, and he pursued his downed opponent.

Most of the people watching stepped closer, drawn by the suspense of the fight, but Ariella could not move. She did not want to see the end.

People's backs blocked her view, and she was bracing herself for the final blow, the deathly scream of pain. Yet suddenly she heard an astounded murmur from the spectators. She pushed her way to the front.

Demetrius was up again, fighting, still untouched by the Koroi blade.

"I've been kept confined most of my life," he said as he advanced, "but one thing a prisoner has is time... time to practice swordplay."

"You think you've practiced enough in your gilded cage?"

Riobard retorted.

"I'll have my blade answer that."

Their swords sang through the air, and Ariella was amazed at their skill. She had never seen Demetrius fight this well. A relentless gleam in his eye, he forced his opponent to retreat. No matter how Riobard tried to sidestep, Demetrius seemed to herd him persistently back. The Koroi chief looked outraged that his skills were failing him, but all he could do was retreat until he found himself backed up against the wooden target to which Demetrius had been tied and assaulted with a hail of arrows only two days ago.

Riobard sidestepped to escape, but just as he did so, his opponent's blade streaked across his shoulder, leaving a thin, red mark.

"First blood," Demetrius said.

He was panting, holding his sword at the ready. He could not be blamed for expecting Riobard to attack him in a fit of rage.

The defeated chief also breathed heavily, leaning back against the target as if the scratch was a mortal wound.

The Koroi were silent. Then one of them shouted, "Well done, Sylcadian." Another man said, "You both fought well." "A good fight! A good fight!" the other Koroi took up the cry.

This seemed to rouse Riobard. He offered his hand and the two fighters exchanged a gesture of good will.

"The woman is yours," Riobard said though it obviously pained him to do so.

"Thank you, Toroi," Demetrius replied as they walked back towards Ariella and Edoline, "You are an honorable man. But I will not hold you to the agreement."

"What?" Riobard pronounced.

"I second that sentiment," Edoline growled, "What?"

Ariella was simply dumbfounded. Perhaps she was not wrong, perhaps he had fought for her after all. She could not allow herself to hope, and even now she pushed that damned emotion down as if it was a pile of refuse.

"I've changed my mind," Demetrius said, "I see how

strongly you feel about Edoline. She is yours."

"I'm... what?"

Edoline's beautiful eyes bulged out of her head.

"Why you double-traitor!" she cried in a complete frenzy, "Rejecting me a second time! I will not take this insult, I will kill you!"

She strove to escape the guards, roaring like a wild animal, and they struggled to restrain her.

Riobard did not stand on ceremony but with a wave of his hand ordered his men to take her away.

"You are free to go too," he said to Demetrius.

"With your permission, Toroi, I will stay here. I have sworn to protect my lady Ariella at all times, and I will not leave her side. I promise there will be no more attempts to take Edoline from you, and I will abide by any other rules you wish to impose on me."

Riobard was taken aback, but he tried to appear the equanimous leader.

"You won the bout," he said, "and you were more than kind in returning Edoline to me. Your request is granted. Now, please stay out of my sight for a while."

Demetrius bowed and at once sought Ariella with his eyes.

She met his gaze. To her surprise, it was not proud but once again vulnerable and pleading just as it had been when he told her he loved her. It would be hard to resist him, now that he determinedly stated his claim to remain in the Koroi camp.

She did not speak to him, but turned and went to seek her tent for the night. She needed to be alone. But Demetrius followed her, and she could feel his gaze as she walked, even more gracelessly than usual, since the events of the evening left her exhausted. Too many things had happened, and she could not make sense of any of it. Demetrius had once again done an unforgivable thing by running away with Edoline, but he now preferred to stay with her. Unless he simply did it because he gave up on being able to escape with his rightful fiancee...

As she reached her tent, she spun around to confront him.

"What is it you want?"

"Nothing," he said, the pleading look now gone, replaced by one of amusement. "I only wish to sleep in my lady's tent."

"That is very bold. You think after tonight's escapade I can readily forgive you?"

"No, not readily, but maybe with time..."

"You tried to escape with that scheming snake. You made me relive everything that happened in Sylcadia."

"That was not my intention. You didn't really believe I would choose her over you? I actually feel terrible about deceiving her. You saw how poorly she reacted when she realized my only true aim was to win you back. Please allow me the privilege to stay in your tent this night. After all, Riobard would be furious if he knew I was running about his camp and getting up to all manner of mischief. He seems to hold you responsible for my actions."

"Now you're blackmailing me! I would never have believed it of you, Demetrius. That is too lowly."

"You force me to stoop to lowly tricks," he countered. "You left me no choice."

"I gave you one choice: to leave my camp. That was what you should have done!"

He shook his head. "I could not do that."

Ariella fumed, but could not think of a way to make him change his mind short of following Riobard's example and trying to fight him in a duel.

But then, if he wanted so badly to stay, she could make his life a living hell.

"You may sleep here," she said, "bearing in mind that sleep is all you'll be doing. I hope you enjoy it. But first... since you claim to be a humble follower of mine, you will groom my horse. I'm sure her coat and her hooves need cleaning."

Demetrius raised one eyebrow. "Well played. I see you're still angry with me."

"I'm not angry, I'm furious. Now go, before I change my mind and trade you to Riobard for a few Koroi daggers."

***

Demetrius tried to gather his thoughts. He walked swiftly, trying to look only at the ground and nothing else. At this moment, he would have punched any man who even so much as breathed at him the wrong way.

He had taken a gamble and made a terrible sacrifice in running away with Edoline only to reveal his devotion to Ariella. He had probably lost Edoline's trust and made a lifelong enemy out of her. But it made no difference. Did Ariella not realize how much he had risked? Had she not seen him fight?

He found the horses and remembered which one was hers, a sleek brown mare. Gradually, he felt calmer as he stroked the horse, whose coat indeed was covered in dust and loose hairs.

"By all the living and antelope-loving stars," he said to the horse, "she won't stop until she drives me mad."

He brushed the horse's coat with care, checked her hooves, and when he finished, decided to brush a couple of other beasts that stood nearby. The earthy smell of the horses and the repetitive motion of his work felt soothing.

His feelings of anger at Ariella's continued rebuffs in the face of his desperate efforts mixed with relief at being able to stay by her side, all were toned down as he worked.

She had never been cruel before. It didn't seem in her nature. So if she was being cruel now, then perhaps she had been hurt so deeply that she believed it was her only way to get back at him. Well, he could stand it. The only thing he wouldn't be able to stand from her was rejection.

When he returned to her tent, Ariella was already lying down, wrapped up in her blanket. Her face turned away from him, she said, "Do not fret over Edoline. Riobard would never force himself on her. He has fanciful ideas about riding with a warrior woman on his side. But once it's all over, you can take her back and marry her."

"I don't want to marry her," he said cheerfully as he lay down at a respectful distance. He stretched his own blanket out and wrapped himself in it, enjoying the restful sensation after a day of considerable activity.

"Then why did you risk your life to escape with her?" Ariella asked, turning to face him.

"You still don't understand..."

"No, I don't. All I understand is you are the most indecisive person I've ever met."

"I'm not indecisive. Absconding with Edoline was part of my plan to win you back."

"A very strange plan indeed," Ariella scoffed.

"At least it was a plan," he argued, "I did something, unlike back in Sylcadia, where I allowed things to linger and fester. You were right to reject me for bringing you there and making you a target of Edoline's jealousy. But I thought if I absconded with Edoline, you would surely try to bring me back. If not for my sake, then maybe for the sake of your alliance with Riobard."

Ariella sat up, looking at him with a perplexed expression.

"And if I didn't?"

"I just hoped you would."

"I see, quite a flawless plan. And did you think what would happen if you got captured, which is in fact what happened?"

"I did," he said proudly, "in fact, I thought the likelihood of being captured was very high. And I hoped you would again negotiate with the chief to defend me, which you did, albeit in a rather cold manner. You risked your alliance for me, you can't deny it. You still care for me."

She tried to make her face impassive, but even in the darkness of the tent, he was aware of the struggle it took.

"You did a brave thing rescuing Edoline, and I commend it. You don't deserve death, that is all."

Had he expected her to fall into his arms and forgive the past so easily? Yes, perhaps he had. But now he knew it would be anything but easy. Still, he saw a sliver of a chance to win her back.

Ariella turned away again, snuggling into her blanket. All he could see was the outline of her hair, tempting him to stroke it.

"Who gave you that scar on your face?" he asked.

"Someone who is dead. The man who forced us to fight is dead too."

Demetrius smiled. "I would expect nothing less." But he knew all too well the grief that could hide beneath such facile words.

"How many fights did I miss?" he asked.

"Too many," she snapped.

"I should have been here by your side. None of this would have happened if I hadn't taken you back to Sylcadia. Believe me, I have so many regrets. I tried to make myself behave like a prince, feel like a prince, but it was unnatural. I came to realize that I am just... myself."

"What a fascinating discovery!" she shot back, "Did you reach it all by yourself or with a council of wizards helping you?"

"I just thought you might be interested to know," he said levelly. "You cared about me once. When I fell ill, was it only a dream, or did you reach me from some strange spirit realm?"

"It doesn't matter," she mumbled. "Now, will you stop talking and let me sleep? I swear, you talk more than any man I've ever met."

"Are you questioning my manliness now?" he asked, not sure whether to be amused or irritated.

"Maybe I am."

"As if I haven't proven it many times. Not least of which tonight. I fought for you."

"Fought for Edoline more like."

"I fought for you, only for you," he said, "And I always will."

Ariella was silent, and he didn't dare pursue the subject. He had said everything he wanted to say, and he could sense that she was still not ready to forgive him or to open up to him.

He had trouble sleeping, and what felt like one or two hours later, he heard Ariella stirring uneasily under her blanket. She uttered a soft cry and flailed her arm. Then she opened her eyes, clearly awaking from a nightmare. Her face looked perturbed for a moment, then she breathed a sigh of relief.

Demetrius risked her displeasure to crawl from beneath his blanket towards hers. He stayed on the other side of the blanket but put his arms around her, seeking to give her comfort, and she did not push him away although she frowned at this breach of etiquette. At first she seemed anxious, her heartbeat frantic, but she calmed and relaxed into him.

"What did you dream about?" he asked.

"Nothing important," she said, "You don't have to hold me."

Yet, she did not struggle from his grasp.

"What was it?"

"It was just... wild dogs attacking me. One of them bit into my arm. That was when I woke up."

"It was only a dream," he said holding her closer.

"I never had so many nightmares before Howell," she muttered.

"Who is that?"

"Another dead man."

Demetrius clenched his jaw in anger, wishing he could have killed Howell himself, whoever he was. There was much he didn't know about what she had gone through, but he would not push her. It was enough that she was talking to him now and letting him stay close by.

"You take no prisoners," he said. "Sooner or later you will defeat all your enemies with or without my help. But I will stay by your side and make sure no one can hurt you again."

"Demetrius—"

"I will wait as long as it takes for you to forgive me. Even if you never do, I will stay with you as your servant if that's what you wish."

"Let us not talk..."

"You're right," he agreed, "Go back to sleep. I'll be here."

She relaxed into him, and soon her breathing levelled out and deepened. It was torture, holding her supple body and being unable to act on his passion. Adding to the ache of his wounds was now the strain of a maddening erection, but at last after so many endless months, he held her in his arms and had no desire to let go.

CHAPTER 18

Awaking beside the man she had both dreamed about and loathed for so many long months was confusing, to say the least. She wanted to run her finger along his jaw and feel the short hair of his beard, to kiss his luxurious eyelashes.

He slept soundly, and the serenity of his perfect, sleeping face lured Ariella into a sense that all would be well.

She did not trust this feeling; past experience had taught her that nothing went smoothly where the two of them were concerned. For all she knew, Edoline could break free and kidnap him, or his mother could raise an army to bring him back to Sylcadia. Besides, she herself had still not forgiven him, though she wanted to more than anything in the world.

Quietly, she slipped from under the blanket and stalked out of the tent. Forgoing breakfast, she sought only solitude and space to think.

She chose the tallest hill of the ones that surrounded the campsite. Her footsteps frightened small lizards, who scurried in all directions, and she enjoyed the exercise of the steep climb. Gradually, a view of the camp and the wilderness beyond stretched out in a wide sweep beneath a clear, azure sky.

At the top of the hill, she realized the solitude she sought was not to be had because Mara sat there. But instead of being disappointed, Ariella felt pleasantly surprised to find her long-lost friend lounging happily on the arid, yellow hillside.

"Come," Mara said in her easy way, patting the dusty rock surface beside her. "You're looking gloomy."

"I spent the night with Demetrius," she blurted out.

"Oh, was it very dull? Good looking men can be the worst in bed. They don't think they need to even try."

Ariella chuckled. "Mara, you are a fountain of knowledge. But it's not that."

She looked out over the small stream gurgling beneath, trying to absorb its calming effect. "I can't forgive him," she said "I don't love him anymore."

"You seem to be loving him just fine by the sounds of it," Mara said with a chuckle.

"Mara!"

"What? You loved him all night, didn't you?"

"That's what I'm trying to tell you, I didn't. He insinuated his way into my tent, and I allowed him only to sleep there, thinking I was punishing him. I ended up mostly punishing myself. My body desires him, but I just don't feel the same way in my heart anymore."

Finally, Mara grew more serious.

"Give it time," she said, "I traveled with him from Sylcadia, and he wouldn't shut up about you. But it's more than that. When I was in the elf lands, I found my way out of madness by learning to see things in a new light. Sometimes I feel things like other people's emotions, sometimes I have visions. When I look at Demetrius, I sense that he will do anything for you, he will become a different person if need be."

Ariella knew it was true. He was already becoming a different person, someone very difficult to contend with.

"He must get this from his mother. Once he has set his mind on something, he will not give up."

"The choice is yours," Mara said, "but don't you give up too soon either."

They talked about the Ringing Woods and all the wonders Mara encountered there. No matter how much distress Ariella experienced with the arrival of Demetrius and Edoline, she was genuinely grateful for Mara's return.

"Can you really go invisible like an elf now?" she asked.

Mara nodded, looking proud. "Evoe and Lorel sort of helped me that time, but I think I could do it in a pinch."

"I blamed myself for ruining your life," Ariella confessed, "Taking you with us on that journey."

"I hope you've stopped that sillyness," Mara said, "There wasn't much life left to ruin by the time you met me. If anything, you have given me a new life. And now I would like to repay what you did for me."

"You already have. Seeing you well again brings me untold happiness."

"I want to do more," Mara replied with such confidence that Ariella felt comforted, "I want to help you get home."

A few more days passed uneventfully. Ariella resumed her training with Jaquelle, though not at such a frenetic pace as before. Sometimes they would ride away from the camp to conceal the magical crystal from prying eyes and practice using it to attack and defend. Most evenings, she dined with Riobard, Mara, and her other companions.

She still allowed Demetrius to sleep in her tent and she wondered when he would grow frustrated enough to either say something about the arrangement or to give up his dream of winning her back. Soon enough, the moment came.

That evening, she was invited again to the tent of the Koroi chief. Just before that, Demetrius caught up with her as she walked to her tent to find something to wear for the evening. He had been sitting nearby, chatting with a few Koroi men, having already made friends quickly here, as was his way.

"Care for some company?" he asked after taking leave of his companions.

"If you like," she shrugged.

They walked on in silence. She noted that he had shaved off his beard, and now the astounding beauty of his face clouded her thoughts. She tried to cling to the reminder of how dishonorably she had acted due to their affair.

"I will drink with Riobard tonight," she announced, "so do not wait for me. I may be with him till the dawn."

"Should I be jealous since you word it like that?" he asked, exquisite dark eyebrows drawing together.

"I would not presume to tell you how to feel," she countered. "But it would be ridiculous to be jealous over me since you and I are in no way connected."

"Aren't we?" he asked, pulling her to face him with sudden vigor.

"Let go of me!" she cried, extricating her arms from his grip.

He obeyed, but in his silence there was a building fury.

"As you like," he finally said without looking at her. "I will ride into town and maybe find someone I can carouse with till the dawn."

"Good!" she shouted as he walked away.

After all the assurances of his love, she did not believe his threat was real. It couldn't be. But suspicion nagged in the back of her mind even as she prepared to see Riobard. She brushed her hair thoroughly and put on a revealing gown which had been sent to her by that meddling rascal, Vidor. It was made of a shimmering fabric, low cut at the front with several slits in the skirt, showing much of her legs. She was not sure why she was doing this. It was not in her plans to seduce the chief, but if something happened, so much the better. She craved some kind of release.

The truth was their drinking together was becoming a habit which Ariella was beginning to enjoy more and more. She also felt it was necessary to put in an appearance after the near disintegration of their alliance due to Demetrius' rash actions.

Neither of them wanted to bring up the recent incident, but they were not hard pressed for other conversation. There was only one attendant in the tent, a very old man, and he poured the whisky at regular intervals. Time seemed to pass quickly, and Ariella was happy to forget all other concerns in conversation with the chief.

"Did you ever wonder why I have no tattoos on my arms unlike all the other Koroi warriors?" Riobard asked.

"Yes, I've been staying up late the past few nights thinking about it," she said mockingly.

She found herself constantly flirting with Riobard. They sat side by side at the small table, and she kept trying to sneak a sideways look at his face.

She felt drawn to the chieftain with a kind of friendship that sometimes unites people of the most different heritage as if they had known each other in a previous life. She could talk to him for hours.

"Well, I shall tell you," he said. "Any warrior who had been in battle should have these tattoos, and I have been in a few. But I have so much faith in conquering the Northern Coast, I declined to have the markings because I will soon become a northern king and will wear a crown instead."

"I like your confidence," Ariella said, this time without mockery.

"I like your anger," he replied.

"Anger?" she asked, confused.

She had grown to like him, but she could not seem to entice him with her outrageous gown. Like most men, he was not unaffected by such displays. His pupils widened at times, but he showed no other signs of taking their alliance a further step. If anything, he had been beyond courteous all evening.

"No, you are not angry with me," he said with a slight chuckle. "But I feel bad for that madman you call your servant."

"Madman?"

"He must be mad to want to suffer all your whims. And you must hate him or love him very much."

"That is not for you to judge," she retorted, "I treat him as he deserves."

"I would like nothing more than to fall in love with you,

Ariella," he suddenly said, taking her completely by surprise.

"But something prevents you?" she asked, fascinated.

"Only that your heart clearly belongs to another. And then, I can always find plenty of other ways to make a fool of myself, as you have clearly witnessed."

"I thought you were someone who avoided making a fool of himself," she pointed out.

"I do try to avoid it, but often fail. But then, we are all full of contradictions," he mused, taking a long drink of liquor. "You like to harp on honor, yet you carry these throwing knives in your cloak."

Ariella was glad they had changed the subject.

"Well, a few extra blades are always helpful," she reasoned.

"Sometimes honor has to be sacrificed for the right thing to be done," Riobard said, "It's not for me to tell you when that is."

"Indeed it's not," she said with mock grandeur, "because I am the commander of our forces."

"I know," he replied as calmly as ever, "That's exactly what I'm trying to tell you. Because aside from being Shonrok and all that, you are a very kind woman. I just don't know if you are prepared for what's to come."

"Of course I'm prepared," she scoffed, "I have been to war before."

"Not just war. You are a rebel now. You will take back your castle and your kingdom without needing anyone's permission. I know you're determined enough to let nothing stop you. This makes your high-faluting concepts of honor... somewhat irrelevant."

Ariella dwelled on his words. She had come to know that Riobard was no fool, and she valued his advice despite pretending to scoff at it. This time, something about that conversation haunted her more than usual as she stumbled back to her tent.

Upon reaching it, she wrapped herself in her cloak, then turned around and went to find her horse. Aside from its glamour, the good thing about her dress was that the high slits in the skirt allowed her to ride in it. It would only take a couple of hours to get to Nor Kemur.

Vidor was one of those people who hardly ever slept, while Demetrius liked to keep late hours and rise late in the morning. So, Ariella was not surprised to find them both still awake at this ridiculous hour and drinking together at the Sprightly Pig.

"When you said you would find someone to carouse with all night, I thought you meant a woman," she announced, walking confidently toward their table.

Demetrius turned to look at her. She liked his gaze, long and admiring, gliding over her body in unmistakable enjoyment. He seemed a little drunk, but she did not care what sort of a state he was in. In fact, his inebriation made his gestures if not his words more honest.

"Vidor was only just telling me about a woman who would suit the purpose," he slurred ever so slightly, "An actress I think it was. For me to carouse... with."

Ariella did not believe a word of it. As she stood before their table, Demetrius' eyes were fastened to her, blue irises aflame.

The other few customers of the tavern did not look at her too shyly either. In all her time here, she had never worn a dress like this.

"I was not!" Vidor objected, sensing that he was in a dangerous spot.

"Vidor," Ariella said, "I am sorry to take your companion away from you, but I must speak to him alone."

"By all means," Vidor said, looking both frightened and intrigued. "Speak to him."

"Now?" Demetrius asked.

"Now. Come with me," she commanded.

In a voice that was soft yet charged with long-suppressed passion, Demetrius said, "Anything my lady wishes."

He got up unsteadily and followed her up the stairs.

The rest of the late-night revellers, who had never seen her take a man up to her room before, now cheered wildly. Accompanied by cries of "The Bride of Death has a suitor!" "Do not fail, Sylcadian!" "Stay strong and don't let it droop!" and the banging of fists and cups on tables, she ignored them, never slowing her stride, not looking back to see if Demetrius was following.

As soon as they were in the small, dark room and the door closed behind them, she pulled Demetrius into a close embrace and kissed him with urgent passion. She drank the scent of spirits from his breath, feeling as intoxicated as he was. The darkness of the chamber seemed to grow denser as his lips and tongue wrung helpless moans from her and the full weight of his body pressed her against the door. He clutched a thick strand of her hair and held it tightly at the nape of her neck as his mouth devoured hers.

"This doesn't mean I forgive you..." she breathed between kisses, "This doesn't mean anything. But I want you."

"I understand," he said, not letting the warning stop him or even slow him down.

His hands planed up and down her thighs frantically. Spearing her mouth with his tongue, he reached his hand under the flimsy gown and delving under the narrow strip of cloth that concealed her sex, touched the wetness between her legs.

She nearly fell over the edge of sanity at his touch. Then his finger delved deeper inside, and she writhed with uncontrolled lust. His other hand squeezed her breast hard, but she wanted him to do it even harder.

"I want you now," she panted, "I want you inside me."

Demetrius lifted her up, and she wrapped her legs around his hips, clinging to him tightly. Never ceasing their kiss, he carried her to the bed, then threw her on it.

"Gently," she chided, but then let one corner of her mouth lift wickedly. "At least, to start."

"Gently?! Will you never stop tormenting me?" he asked, divesting her of her clothes with impatience.

"Never," Ariella laughed.

Guilt at using him thus without giving him hope for the future only added fuel to her need. The more decadent impulses of her soul begged to be released, to run riot and she allowed them to.

Demetrius flung off his own clothes as if they were poisonous. The only things covering him now was one bandage on his arm and a few more around his torso.

The tension in his face testified to how much control he was exerting not to take her like a wild stallion mounting a mare.

He entered her excruciatingly slowly, extending the pleasure of that first stroke to an endless moment. Perhaps that was what she loved most about making love to him. He obeyed her perfectly in every way, and he took pleasure in it despite what he said. He might have been able to overpower her with brute strength, but he seemed to prefer conquering her with soft kisses.

Each time he dipped forward again and again with deliberate slowness. Her fingernails raked his shoulders as she groaned with pleasure. The slow rhythm was unbearable, yet so ecstatic.

But soon he lost all semblance of gentleness, and Ariella was glad of it. His manhood pounded into her body with savage force. She could not quite read his face, taut with lust, but also what seemed like anger. Her hips responded with an equal measure of both.

She knew when he was close to the edge... The pulsing inside her grew even more intense, even hotter. All she could feel was amazement at how good it felt when he came, taking her along with him.

For a while, all she could do was stare at the ceiling, unseeing and uncomprehending. All she could feel was her heartbeat drumming throughout her body and the undeniable waves of soft pleasure lingering in her limbs. It took a long time for her breath to slow to something resembling normal.

She took one look at Demetrius, seeing that he had not completely recovered, but she straddled him anyway.

She curled her fingers around his shaft and rubbed herself against it. They both gasped with the sudden sensation.

The pleasure of rubbing against his hardness made her forget everything else. She moved her hips rhythmically, faster and faster. It was only when he whispered, "Yes, use me," that she realized he was enjoying it too.

He grew harder beneath her touch.

"You are nothing but my plaything," she said, not slowing her rhythm.

"Yes," he breathed.

She felt him grow even harder as his powerful chest heaved with every breath.

She hardly knew what she was saying or doing. All she wanted now was to be filled by him again. She brought him into her pliant wetness, savoring every inch of him.

Her fingers captured his hair, while her other hand braced against his chest as she arched her back. Demetrius' hands held her hips, urging her to a faster rhythm.

As she looked down at him, the languid yet ardent look in his eyes as he watched her work herself up into a frenzy, she felt so beautiful and so desired. His hands moved together with her hips as one.

She drew him into the maelstrom of ultimate pleasure when she felt her center contract to what felt like a tiny point, then release powerful currents of ecstasy. She could faintly hear his groans mixed with her own.

Then she collapsed onto his chest. The feel of his skin, his scent, the roughness of his cheek against hers, all of this in its own way was perhaps just as pleasurable as the heights she had just experienced.

"The beard was nice, but this is better," she said, stroking the stubble on his cheek.

"So all it took was shaving off my beard? A small sacrifice. And here I had feared I might never have the chance to experience this again."

"Was it good then?" she asked in her usual careless manner.

"It's always good with you," he replied tenderly.

Ariella felt an uncomfortable silence building up. She did not trust this situation enough to talk to him like they had in the past, like lovers.

"But really... what caused this change of heart?" Demetrius said at length.

"I spoke with Riobard."

Demetrius chuckled, and she felt the reverberations of sound from his chest, a pleasant vibration against her skin.

"Did he have some words of wisdom from the honorable Bai Meng?"

"Yes, he did, though I don't think he was talking about us."

"Another riddle worthy of Bai Meng. What does it mean?"

"I'm a rebel now, commanding a rebel army," she responded, lifting her head to look into his sky-blue eyes, "and the thing about rebels is... they take what they want."

Some other man might have found these words insulting, but he did not. Ariella could tell by the way his eyes flared up with passion on hearing this utterance.

He said, "Then take me, rebel lady."

OTHER TITLES BY CAROLEE CROFT

Belinda's Revenge

Belinda is an innocent but impetuous young lady who enjoys card games, flirting and gossip. But her world is about to be turned upside down by the forces of passion...

When the lovelorn Baron Robert Petre cuts off a lock of her hair without her permission, putting her reputation in jeopardy, Belinda is beyond furious. Just as she was beginning to love him, she feels violated and betrayed...

Luckily, Belinda has the Sylphs to assist her. With the help of these supernatural spirits, she kidnaps the baron and imprisons him in a remote hunting cabin. He is chained naked to a four-poster bed, completely helpless, with no choice but to submit to her fiery desires...

What Belinda doesn't know is that her escapades could soon become the talk of London thanks to an untrustworthy friend. Can Belinda and Robert find forgiveness in their hearts before it's too late?

Engaged to the Earl

At twenty one, Martha Darrington was hoping that she still had several years of carefree cavorting ahead of her. She thinks that her time in Bath is only a restful holiday. However, she is shocked to find that her strict aunt has arranged her engagement to the Earl of Bradfield.

Edward would like nothing more but to continue his affair with the possessive Elizabeth Camplyon, while entering into a loveless marriage of convenience with Martha. Seeing that her future husband is not attracted to her, Martha turns to her steadfastly loyal servant Tom for affection. When her wedding is imminent, she tries to win the earl's love using a magic potion, but the plan backfires... in a most sexy way.

Uniform Desire

Do you get a buzz from seeing a lover in uniform? Uniform Desire is packed with stories for uniform loving romance readers! From taboo sex to modern day threesomes, from a werewolf to a firefighter, there's something for everyone in this anthology of eleven very different sexy, kinky stories!

The Stars at Zenith Trilogy:

Ariella's Escape

Ariella's Rebellion

Ariella's Nemesis

ABOUT THE AUTHOR

Carolee Croft enjoys traveling around the world, trying chocolate in all its various forms, and relaxing with a good book. She is obsessed with Italian greyhounds.

Connect with Carolee online:

http://caroleecroft.wordpress.com
@CaroleeCroft
http://www.facebook.com/caroleecroft/

Ariella's Rebellion